Just Grace

.....

Still Just Grace

.....

Just Grace Walks the Dog

Read about all of Grace's adventures in these books:

Just Grace

· · · · ·

Still Just Grace

· · · · ·

Just Grace
Walks the Dog

Written and illustrated
by
Charise Mericle Harper

HOUGHTON MIFFLIN COMPANY

Boston New York

The illustrations in this book are pen-and-ink drawings
digitally colored in Photoshop.
The text of this book is set in Dante.

Library of Congress Cataloging-in-Publication Data for individual titles is on
file.

ISBN: 978-0-544-85453-6

Manufactured in the United States
DOC 10 9 8 7 6 5 4 3 2 1
4500595055

CONTENTS

CHERRY

CRINKLES

Me

BUG

Just Grace

For My Mother,
who is full of grace.

I Did Not Get To Be

1 I did not get to be the helper to Mister Magic the Magician at my very own (so it should have been me) sixth birthday party because Sammy Stringer spit purple grape juice all over my special white shirt with a big six on it, and I had to change it right when Mister Magic was starting up.

Mom said she was sure it was an accident, but I just know that spitting is pretty much an on-purpose thing, and it is almost impossible to forgive someone for something on purpose even if it was almost three years ago, which is a very long time.

Before After It Doesn't even look like a "6" Anymore.

2 I did not get to be a singing and dancing corncob in the Thanksgiving play because I was the only girl tall enough to fit into the tree costume who didn't cry real boo-hoo baby tears when she was asked, "Could you please not be a corncob, because what we really, really need is a tree and we already have way more than enough corn-cobs."

I will not say who cried big tears, and is probably a good actress because two seconds after she found out I was going to be the tree she was all smiles, because I am not a tattletale-type person. But I will say that I do not like her even one tiny bit, and that when she is not doing her acting, her true self is a Big Meanie!

Mom said I was a great tree even though I didn't get to say any-thing and Mr. Franks kept whispering at me

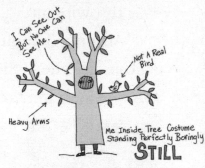

I Can See Out But No One Can See Me.

Not A Real Bird

Heavy Arms

Me Inside Tree Costume Standing Perfectly Boringly **STILL**

to stop moving my arm branches around so much—he didn't think it should be a

Fun Streamer With Real Pieces of Corn on The end.

The Singing And Dancing CornCob looks Beautiful!

windy day. But if you are a tree it is boring to stand there super still with your arms out on each side doing nothing.

3 I did not get to be in the talent night at school and show off the photos I took with my new camera because I was sick with the stomach flu and was throwing up.

my Special Red Bucket. I only use it to Throw Up in when I am sick.

Aurora Gambit won a first-prize blue ribbon for her photos of flowers, which were okay, but my cat photos are way better

and would have for sure taken her first-prize ribbon right away. Plus, she could be happy with the second-prize ribbon because it is red and that is one of her favorite colors because she says that red things look good with her orangish hair.

ONE OF MY GREAT CAT PHOTOS

Sammy Stringer got an honorable mention green ribbon for his paintings of dog poop, which is totally unbelievable and gross!

4 But the **biggest** I-did-not-get-to-be of my life, ever, happened right at school in front of everybody in the whole third grade class. I did not get to be called Grace, which is an okay thing if your name is Tania or Ruth or Jordan but totally 100 percent unfair if you are me and your name is Grace, which mine is.

I didn't tell Mom because I knew she'd be mad and call the school, and you can't have your mom call the school unless something really bad happens, like maybe someone mean pushes you down and it breaks three of your front teeth, or else everybody will think you are a big baby and a complainer. And I am not either of those two things!

FOUR GRACES IN A ROW

Grace W. Grace L. Me Grace F.
BIG Meanie!

There are four girls named Grace in my class. Miss Lois, our new teacher, said, "We'll have to do something about that. It's too confusing with all you Graces."

Then she said, "Grace Wallace, you will be Grace W. Grace Francis can be Grace F., and Grace Landowski can be Grace L."

Right then Grace L. stood up and said, "Pretty please, Miss Lois, can I be Gracie instead of Grace L.?"

I knew I was next, so I said, "And I want to be just Grace."

"Perfect," said Miss Lois, and then she went down the list of everyone's new names and wrote them in her special book.

"Let's see, we have Grace W., Grace F., Gracie, and Just Grace."

Then Grace F. stood up and started waving her arm like a crazy person, trying to get Miss Lois's attention. She gave me a mean look and said, "How come she gets to be called Grace and I have to be Grace F.? It's not fair! I want to be the one called Grace!" Miss Lois seemed a little grumpy that we were still talking about the Grace name thing.

She Has Big Ears Like A Monkey. She can Probably Hear Really Good.

She made a big sigh and said, "You're right, dear—it's not fair for anyone to be called Grace, so that's why Grace Stewart wants to be called Just Grace."

Both Grace F. and I said "Just Grace?" at the same time.

"That's weird!" said Grace F.

I tried to tell Miss Lois that she'd made a mistake and that I wanted to be called just **Grace,**

not **Just Grace,** but she put her hand up in the air and said, "That's enough, girls. Let's move on to the three Owens." And that's how it happened that I have the stupidest name in the whole class! Or maybe even the whole entire world!

Boy Things

1 Spitting and making burping noises.

2 Not caring that your shirt or pants are sticky with food or mud or worse...mucus.

3 Really liking big and flashy superheroes
. . . the kind with capes.

4 Drawing comics.

There are some girls who do boy things
and don't care who knows it. Ruth, a girl in
my class from last year, always makes huge
burps after she drinks milk. Everyone says it's
gross, but you can tell that some of the boys
are really impressed, especially Sammy
Stringer—he's always trying to learn stuff to
become more disgusting.

Then there are other girls who might do boy things but don't want anyone to know. I'm one of those. I don't spit, make burp sounds, or wear disgusting filthy clothes, but when I feel grumpy or sad, it sometimes makes me feel better if I draw a comic. I don't know why it works that way, but it does, and that seems like a good thing.

The day I got my Just Grace name I needed to feel better really fast, so I drew a new Not So Super adventure as soon as I got home. It would have been better to watch an episode of *Unlikely Heroes,* but I'm not allowed to watch TV before dinner.

Not So Super comics are about superheroes who only have little powers, but still they use them to help people who need it. I got the idea from my favorite TV show in the whole world, *Unlikely Heroes.* Mimi, my best friend ever, says that *Unlikely Heroes* is the kind of show that makes you want to be a better person just by watching it, which is true, and important.

NOT So SuPER BUT STILL GOOD

My other boy thing is that I sort of have a teeny tiny superpower. It's not a jump-over-buildings, see-through-people's-clothes, or lift-a-train-over-my-head one, which is good, because when you can do those kinds of things you probably have to live in a secret hideout instead of at home with your mom and dad. And I really like my room, so it would be sad to have to move away, so I'm glad I only have a small superpower.

My power is that I can always tell when someone is unhappy, even if that person is pretending to be happy and is a really good actor.

The bad thing about my power is that I always try to do something to make the sad person feel better—even if I should probably leave it alone and not do anything at all. Dad says that feeling people's sadness is called empathy and it's a superpower because of the "having to do something to help them feel better" part. A superhero **has** to help people in trouble. She can't just change into a regular I'm-not-going-to-do-anything-to-help-someone-else type of person even if she wanted to.

**THIS WOULD NEVER HAPPEN
WITH A REAL SUPERHERO**

Rooms You Can Jump In, In My House

1 The bathroom with the broken toilet. Very yucky room.

2 The laundry room. Sometimes when

Mom thinks I have too much energy she tells me to go and jump in the laundry room. I tell her it's no fun to jump in there, plus it's too small. She says, "Why do you have to swing your arms when you jump? There's plenty of room if you jump like a pencil." Then we both laugh because who ever saw a jumping pencil, and she is just being ridiculous.

The reason you can only jump in these two places is that every other room is right above Augustine Dupre's head. Augustine Dupre is the super-amazing French lady who lives in our basement—only the part she lives in doesn't look like a basement, it's a fabulously fantastic apartment.

Dad said she could paint her apartment any way she liked, so she did. Augustine Dupre is not afraid of color. She has a yellow kitchen, an orange bathroom, and a rose-colored bedroom with bright red velvety curtains. It is most truly the coolest place someone could ever live. Dad even bought her apartment a dishwasher, so she doesn't have to wash or dry her dishes by hand like we do.

Augustine Dupre is two times lucky: not only does she have the best apartment ever, but she also has the best job. She is a flight attendant for rich people who travel on airplanes in first class. She could probably go anywhere, but she says her favorite place in the entire whole world is France. Sometimes she even goes there two times in one week.

THAT MEANS GOODBYE IN FRENCH.

AU REVOIR.

Mom says not to bother Augustine Dupre with every little thing that's happening in my life, but it's hard not to tell her stuff, because she's a really good listener.

The day I got my Just Grace name I wanted to run downstairs and tell Augustine Dupre all about it right away, but Mom wouldn't let me. Mom said Augustine Dupre was probably tired from flying home from France.

MOM'S SILLY IDEA

OH MY POOR ARMS! THEY ARE SO TIRED. I JUST FLEW IN FROM FRANCE

After dinner I snuck downstairs when Mom wasn't watching. I did my special knock so Augustine Dupre would know it was me. After I told her all about my stupid new name, she said something in French that sounded like she was feeling the empathy thing for me. Then she said that if I wanted she could tell me a very sad story, and that sometimes hearing a very sad story makes your own sad story seem less sad.

I said I wanted to hear it, because I was desperate to feel better about being Just Grace. Sometimes, not knowing what you are asking for can be a mistake. This might have been one of those times.

The Sad Story

Augustine Dupre's story was all about Mrs. Luther, which was a huge surprise. Mrs. Luther is my next-door neighbor and a teacher from my school. A scary old-kid teacher. Dad says that if something scares you it's probably because you don't know all the facts, and that if you learned more facts then you would not be so scared anymore. Dad is wrong!

What I Know About Mrs. Luther The Teacher

1 Wears her glasses on the end of her nose.

2 Teaches the older kids anthropology, which has something to do with understanding strange people from other countries that no one has probably ever heard of before.

3 Looks at you like she has x-ray eyeballs and can see right through to your bones.

4 Has a funny crooked smile, like a

crocodile that has just eaten something cute and furry.

Mrs. Luther

CROCODILE With Mrs. Luther's Hairstyle and Glasses

5 Has just started wearing a big bright orange cast on her leg, so now she walks around holding on to an old-people cane. Bright orange is not a normal grown-up person's color.

What I Know About Mrs. Luther The Neighbor

6 Her house is full of scary-looking masks

hanging all over the walls. I know this because I can see into her living room from my bedroom window. She never closes her drapes, which is not good for me. Creepy masks are not something I like to see at night before I go to sleep, so I always close my eyes while I pull down my window shade.

7 As soon as she gets home from school she puts on a long dress—like a witch dress but it has more colors.

That's seven strange things instead of five. So because Mrs. Luther is my neighbor, I know she is stranger and scarier than the kids at school would ever guess, because they don't even know about her witch dress or the scary masks on her wall. The only not unusual thing I know about Mrs. Luther is her cat, Crinkles. Crinkles is a very nice cat.

I told Augustine Dupre that I thought Mrs. Luther was unusual, which is a word grownups use to mean weird and strange so they won't hurt anyone's feelings, and that it would probably take a lot for me to feel sad for her, even with my extra-sensitive empathy feelings. Augustine Dupre said she was not worried.

What Augustine Dupre Told Me

1 That Mrs. Luther fell off a ladder in her house while she was trying to hang up a new scary mask and almost squashed Crinkles. This is how she broke her leg and why she has to wear a cast. But this does not explain why it is bright orange instead of a normal grown-up color like white or black.

2 That her son who she loves lives in another country and doesn't call her very much. This is no surprise, because boys do not like to talk on the phone as much as girls.

3 That Mrs. Luther was going to run in a big race and now she can't because she has a broken leg. It is hard to imagine Mrs. Luther wearing a jogging suit, but I don't think she could probably run very fast in her colored witch dress.

4 That her cat, Crinkles, her best friend in the whole world, is now scared of her because he was almost squished by her big bottom when she fell off the ladder, plus he doesn't like the new orange cast. Augustine Dupre said Mrs. Luther is so sad about this that she cries real tears almost every single night.

The first three things didn't make me feel sad even though missing the big race sounded a lot like my missing my talent night, which was sad for me but I'm not old so it's still okay for me to cry when things like that happen. Old people know how to keep their crying feelings inside. They only let them out when something really bad has happened and they are 100 percent sad. This is why just thinking of Mrs. Luther crying in her house with all those scary masks looking down at her made me feel a little bit sad.

And when Crinkles suddenly jumped on Augustine Dupre's windowsill I got even sadder, because Crinkles is such a lovable cat, and if you had the love of such a great cat it would for sure make you feel the sadness-of-everything-in-the-whole-world not to have it anymore.

Crinkles meowed and meowed until Augustine Dupre went to the window and opened it. She put her finger up to her mouth and made a "shhhh" sound. Crinkles wasn't at all shy. He walked in and jumped right up onto her lap. Augustine Dupre pointed her shushing finger at the ceiling, and I knew exactly what she meant.

One of Dad's big rules is No Pets In The Apartment. He wouldn't even let Augustine

Dupre put a bird feeder outside her window. He said it attracted all the messy neighborhood beasts. He would not be happy to know that Crinkles was a visitor. Sometimes people can be rule breakers if the rules are not good ones and the person who made the rules is not an official-type rule maker who wears a uniform—Dad is not one of those.

Augustine Dupre sighed one of her French sighs (my French teacher at school does this too, so I know it is a French thing) and said, "I don't know how we can make poor Mrs. Luther not so sad. In six weeks when her orange cast comes off, I am sure Crinkles will not be scared of her anymore. Then they will love each other again."

"Is she going to cry every night for six weeks?" I couldn't believe that her sadness could be so big.

Augustine Dupre patted my arm and shook her head, which is a grown-up way of saying, "Yes, I'm sorry to say it, but I believe this to be true."

Superhero Mode

That night before going to bed I looked out my window. I could see Mrs. Luther sitting in one of her big chairs, with all her scary masks looking down at her. I couldn't tell if she was crying. Augustine Dupre was right. I was feeling much less sad about being Just Grace. And even though I am not French, I made a French sigh and thought, *I wonder how I can help Mrs. Luther?* This is how my superhero empathy thing always gets started ... and once it is going, there is nothing I can do to stop it.

Breakfast

When I am feeling like a superhero I like to have French toast for breakfast; otherwise I just eat a bagel or cereal. If Mom were a detective she would say, "How come you're always up to something when we have French toast for breakfast?" But she isn't, so she says, "French toast? That's a nice change. We haven't had French toast since that time your dad broke his toe."

When I got to school I could totally see what the disgusting Sammy Stringer had had for breakfast. It was all over his yellow shirt.

"What's the matter? Do you want

some?" He pointed to a brown sticky part and made smacking sounds with his lips.

I gave him my best I-wish-you-would-melt-into-a-puddle-of-goo look and walked away. Mimi and I have been practicing different looks, because you never know when you might need one. You always have to be ready!

"Just Grace, Just Grace, you are so . . ." Sammy probably couldn't think of a rhyme because he was quiet for too many seconds and then he said, ". . . green."

Green isn't even something silly or clever or funny—it is nothing. So what if I was wearing a green shirt? How Sammy Stringer can be so annoying all the time is a question I will never be able to answer! Sometimes I look at him and I can't help it, but I feel like I hate him and feel a little bit sorry for him both at the same time. I don't like it when the inside parts of you don't match up with what the brain part of you thinks. If there were a medicine to make this go away I would take it, even if it was cherry flavor, which tastes terrible and is not my favorite.

What We Are Studying In School That Is Fun

1 Maps and how to draw them—the made-up kind.

MAP OF MY FRIENDS

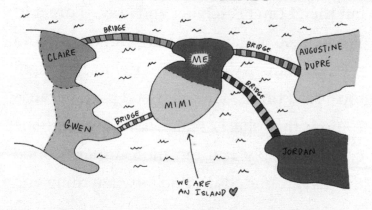

IF THIS WERE A REAL MAP, SAMMY STRINGER WOULD BE SOMEWHERE REALLY FAR AWAY, LIKE OUTER SPACE.

Mimi and I are, of course, best friends, plus we live right next door to each other, so that makes the best friend part even more perfect. Jordan is my best friend in gym class, and she is almost the fastest runner in the whole grade. This is not a good thing if you are "it" and you have to try to catch her. You might think that a real friend would let you catch her sometimes, especially if you are so tired that your eyes might disappear into the back of your head, but Jordan is not that kind of friend. She says, "Try harder." And I do, but then I can't catch her and I say, "Forget it! What is so great about tag anyway?" And then Jordan says, "You're right. I'm tired too." And this is her real friend part, because I know that she is really not tired and she could probably run ten more times around the playground, but I don't say anything and she doesn't say anything and we both sit together and this is good because I am breathing so hard I might almost faint.

Claire is my friend who moved far away, all the way to the ocean. But we can still be friends even though now she lives in California. California is a very beautiful place filled with lots of wonderful things, so I would for sure like to visit her there. She sent me a card and a picture of her standing next to a tree with real oranges on it in her very own backyard. I did not know that oranges grew that way, so there is a lot to learn in California. I am hoping I can visit her some-time soon and miss school. My teachers could not get grumpy and mad about that since I would still be doing lots of learning, only about new California things, which would for sure be much more fun and exciting than regular school learning.

Gwen is Mimi's cousin. I just put her on the map because when she visits Mimi and we are together she is my friend too.

2 Graphs—sort of like percentages if they were in a picture.

3 Percentages—which I already kind of know about from watching *Unlikely Heroes*. They always say things like, "The chance this could happen again is .006 percent," which is like saying almost probably never in a hundred years.

What We Are Studying In School That Is Not Fuh

1 The names of all fifty states and where

they are on the map, which is too many to remember even when they are in a song that is supposed to be fun but is not.

2 Spelling, spelling, and more spelling.

3 The life cycle of frogs, which I do not like because they are slimy and one of Sammy Stringer's favorite creatures.

4 The life cycle of a cucumber, which is not exciting for me because I do not like cucumbers or even pickles, which are like tiny cucumbers and maybe even the babies of big cucumbers, but they are still not nice or tasty to eat.

CUCUMBER

I AM FILLED WITH HORRIBLE SEEDS!

FIVE BABIES, WHICH ARE CALLED PICKLES.

I told Mimi all about Mrs. Luther and Crinkles. She is my only friend who knows about the empathy superhero thing. She knows about it so much that she said, "What are you going to do about it?" right when I finished telling her the story.

Sometimes she likes to help out with projects. She says she is happy to just be the helper because if something goes wrong she probably won't get in as much trouble as the leader, which is me.

I didn't have a big plan to tell her about, so I said, "What do you think we should do?"

Sometimes Mimi has good ideas too. She said, "I think we should go to my house and watch *Unlikely Heroes* so we can get some inspirations." *Unlikely Heroes* is her favorite show too. I knew she'd think of something. Plus, Mimi's mom and dad don't have a rule

that says no TV before dinner. Super super
great!

Supergirl

After school we went to Mimi's house, which
is almost like me walking home but then just
going next door instead. We practiced some
looks, like the I-can't-believe-you-said-that
look and the I-think-you-are-disgusting look
on each other for a while, and then we
watched *Unlikely Heroes*.

This is the most amazing show you could
ever watch. Every week they show real live
normal people who do superhero things.
Once there was a man who lifted a whole car
off a lady who was trapped underneath, and
then there was a baby who didn't even know
how to talk yet but dialed 911 emergency

when his mom fainted on the floor. These people are just regular everyday people who suddenly get superpower brains or energy. The bad part for them is that instead of getting to keep the powers all the time they only have them for a little while, like maybe five seconds or ten minutes, and then they are back to being just regular normal no-power people.

The unbelievable best thing is that all the stories are 100 percent really true. Mom says it's a feel-good show, which means that you feel better just watching it. Dad says feel-good shows aren't very popular and that one day soon it will probably be canceled off the TV. I just can't understand why that would happen, but we tape every episode so if it does we can still watch them forever and ever.

Of course we had to watch our favorite episode, where a girl makes a rope out of her clothes and helps pull a grown-up man out of a river before he sinks to the bottom and drowns. She is a hero and only wearing her underwear. The extra-amazing thing is that she just by accident wore her Supergirl undershirt and underpants that day. That makes her being a hero even more I-can-hardly-believe-it!

← SUPER GIRL UNDERWEAR

↖ SHE DIDN'T HAVE TO TAKE HER SOCKS OR SHOES OFF.

When it was time for me to go home for supper we still didn't have any good ideas. Mimi even put on her Supergirl T-shirt for inspiration—which is a big word for something that helps make you think of the exact right thing you were hoping to think of—but it wasn't working. I don't have any Supergirl clothes. Not even Supergirl underwear, and I really, really, really want some of those. I could wear them for inspiration thinking and no one would even know. Mom says she is keeping her eye out for them, but that Supergirl underwear isn't that easy to find. I think she is just not trying very hard!

Ways To Not Get A Good Idea

1 Ask your mom or dad.

2 Look in a book that has ideas about how to get ideas.

3 Sit down and think super hard about getting a good idea.

I had tried all of those things at other times and none of them had worked even one tiny bit . . . especially number three. Sometimes it is better to try to just do normal things instead of thinking really hard about getting an idea. Then after a while, the start of a good idea might just pop into your head right at the moment you aren't even thinking about it. It is not good to be thinking, *Is the good idea going to happen in the next two minutes?* That doesn't work either.

Start Of My Big Idea

We had supper and then when we were clearing the table Mom said, "Oh, I forgot to tell you. You got a postcard today. It's on the desk in the hall." How Mom could forget something exciting like a postcard but remember boring things like how many bites of green beans I eat and if I remember to put the toilet lid down is something I hope I'm never going to understand. This is one of the reasons I am not so excited about turning into a grownup. The grown-up world is very filled up with boring rules about eating and cleaning.

The card was from Auntie Bethany. She always sends a postcard when she goes some-where fun. I like that she is thinking of me when she is having a big adventure. Postcards are the best!!!! It makes my insides feel good to get one. Mom says postcards are old-fash-ioned. Some old things can be a good idea. Postcards are one of those things. Right when I was reading the part about Auntie Bethany riding a donkey down the Grand Canyon I got the beginning of a good idea. I should send Mrs. Luther postcards, and they should be from...

This is What Happens When you Get A Big Idea.

This was the part of the idea that wasn't finished. Who could send the card? I don't know anybody that Mrs. Luther would want to get a card from. It wouldn't be so fun to get a card from me... I just live right next door and that is not exciting at all. Who does Mrs. Luther love? Who does she love that I even know? The only answer is Crinkles, but Crinkles is not a person, he is a cat. Cats do not go on exciting holidays, and cats do not write postcards. They can't write anything, even if you helped them and taped a marker to their paw, which would not be such a nice thing to do to a cat that you liked.

Then right when I was thinking about

the marker and the tape I got the rest of the idea. It was perfect. Perfect for me and perfect for Mrs. Luther. It was like a great big Band-Aid. It would fix everything until Mrs. Luther got her cast off.

MR. BAND-AID

My Big Idea

I will send Mrs. Luther postcards from Crinkles, only I will write them and pretend that they are from Crinkles. I will not tape a marker to his paw! Mrs. Luther will be so happy to think that Crinkles is thinking of her even if she really knows for real that it is only pretend, it will make her smile her crocodile smile.

How To Do The Big Idea

1 Take a professional-looking photo of Crinkles and get it blown up big to real cat size. Glue the big photo onto a piece of cardboard. Augustine Dupre can help with this part because she is really good at projects and she will probably be able to make Crinkles sit still so I can take his picture and not have it be all blurry.

2 Take cardboard Crinkles around to different places in town and take his photo there. If I do a good job it will look like the real Crinkles was there instead of the cardboard pretend Crinkles. This will be super cool and funny, because the real Crinkles would never pose in a shopping cart at the grocery store, which is already one of my good ideas about where to take a photo.

3 Glue the photo of cardboard Crinkles onto another piece of cardboard to make a real from-the-store-looking postcard. There is a lot of glue and cardboard in this project, and that makes me worried because it is always hard to get glue to stick in the exact right place you want it to and not have it go all over your fingers or in your hair instead.

4 Mail the postcard, which will not be so hard to do, because Mom has lots of stamps.

I couldn't wait to tell Augustine Dupre all about it. I couldn't wait to hear Mimi say, "Great idea!" I couldn't wait to get started. Too bad it was bedtime.

Superhero Morning

It definitely had to be another French toast breakfast. It takes more than 976 and probably less than 2,000 steps to get to school. I try to count them every morning but always get my attention taken away by something else before I finish. This morning I caught up to Mimi at step number 356, which was okay because it is much more important and fun to talk to her than count steps. She loved my idea and said she couldn't wait to be my helper. She said she is glad I am going to use a cardboard cat because she is very allergic to real cats, which is something I had 100 percent forgotten.

We saw Sammy Stringer and it was too bad but he saw us also. He was riding his bike and delivering newspapers instead of going to school, which is not surprising because our newspaper is always late and Dad usually has to take it on the train with him instead of reading it at breakfast like he likes to do. "Hey, Just Grace, I just delivered your paper." We pretended we didn't hear him. It wasn't fair to call me Just Grace when there weren't even any other Graces around. It was him just being mean and unfair!

Sometimes if Sammy delivers the paper before I leave for school Dad will make me go out to the driveway and get it. I always put on one of Mom's yellow dishwashing gloves first because Sammy is a nose picker and that is disgusting, and you can never tell—he might have done that thing right before he touched our paper.

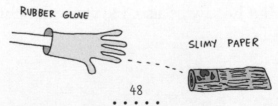

RUBBER GLOVE

SLIMY PAPER

48
· · · · ·

What Happened At School That Was Interesting

1 Mimi had five little tiny sandwiches for lunch instead of one normal-size sandwich. Sometimes little things that are exactly the same as big things are more special and cute (except pickles).

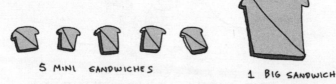

5 MINI SANDWICHES   1 BIG SANDWICH

2 Mrs. Luther had a Band-Aid on her nose, which is something that your eyes have to notice right away. Mimi said she heard that a paperboy had thrown a newspaper at Mrs. Luther's house and that it had hit her in the nose by mistake. And even though it was supposed to be an accident there was no big surprise for me about who the paperboy was. It was Sammy Stringer. Mom said she thought she once saw him try to hit a squirrel with our paper . . . but squirrels are fast. Poor slow Mrs. Luther didn't stand a chance, especially with her broken leg.

SQUIRREL WITH RUNNING SHOES ON

I ran almost all the way home from school. I usually don't have time to count the steps on the way back. I was disappointed that Augustine Dupre wasn't home, but I saw Crinkles sitting under her window. He let me pet him. Too bad I didn't have my camera right then, because he looked extra nice with the sun shining on his fur. Good photographers like to take pictures with real sunlight and not use the flash part of the camera, which is mostly used for inside photos anyway.

HOW TO TAKE A PROFESSIONAL PHOTO

DON'T TAKE A PHOTO OF THE SUN.

SUN IS BEHIND THE PHOTOGRAPHER'S HEAD. THIS IS GOOD.

This is something I learned in the photography book I am reading. It is a very hard book with lots of big words so I usually only read the parts under the pictures. Dad said he is very impressed that I am reading a book from his grown-up book collection.

What Happened At Home That Was Completely Surprising

I was looking out my kitchen window while I was waiting for Augustine Dupre to get home and I saw Sammy Stringer walk up to Mrs. Luther's door. He pushed the door buzzer and then got invited into her house! I ran up to my room and looked out my window, but I couldn't see them in her living room. What he was doing in her house was not something I could even imagine. It was bizarre, which is what they say on *Unlikely Heroes* when something is too hard and not really possible to even understand. I didn't want to think about it, because this kind of thinking usually makes my head hurt, so I drew a new Not So Super comic to try to get my wondering energy away from it.

NOT SO SUPER BUT STILL GOOD

I was so busy drawing, I forgot to notice
when Augustine Dupre came home. And

then it was dinnertime and too late to sneak down to see her.

Mom says she doesn't understand French people, and this is true, because she does not get Augustine Dupre. She understands the words she says but she doesn't know why she says them. Mom says it's a cultural thing, which means that if someone is from another part of the world and you are from here then they might say things that you don't expect, and then you will be confused. I think Mom is wrong, because I can totally understand Augustine Dupre and I have never been to France.

Like the time I gave Augustine Dupre a fake present. I wrapped a lollipop in ten boxes and

Fancy Bow

Lollipop in 10 Boxes

when she finally got to the end, the last wrapper said "Sucker!"

When Mom found out she got mad and said that it wasn't nice to fool someone that way. She made me go downstairs and apologize, and even though I didn't want to I kind of cried. Augustine Dupre said it was all right and I knew she was telling the truth because she once said, "I'll give you ten dollars if you can whistle in the next two minutes while eating these five crackers." I tried and tried but there is no way you can whistle with a mouth full of salty crackers, so she knows how to play a joke too!

THIS IS SOMETHING YOU CANNOT DO

It is much easier to go downstairs and visit when Mom is busy making supper. After dinner she has more time to be watching what I am doing. But tonight I was lucky. Her favorite crime show was on and it was one of those loud noisy ones with lots of sirens, crying, and shooting. She didn't pay any attention to me when I snuck down-stairs.

I told Augustine Dupre all about Sammy Stringer, all about Mrs. Luther, and all about my big idea. She said she was in love with my idea and that she would of course be happy to help me. The whole time we talked about it she was petting Crinkles. That cat has given all his Mrs. Luther love to Augustine Dupre. You can just tell it by the way he looks at her when she scratches him behind his ears. He is filled with love for her . . . poor

Mrs. Luther is definitely triple-wounded.

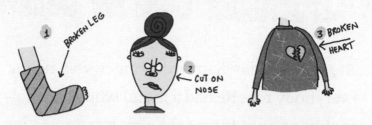

Today it was raining, which was bad and good. Bad because I couldn't take a professional-looking photo of Crinkles outside with the sun shining down on his fur, but good because I am happy to know that Sammy Stringer will have to ride his bike in the rain and get soaking wet while he is delivering papers. This is not just me being mean—he deserves to be wet and unhappy! Plus, the rain will wash away any disgusting germs he leaves on the plastic newspaper bag before anyone else has to touch it! But I will still wear my rubber glove, just to be safe.

What I Almost Could Not Believe

At school today Sammy Stringer was telling everybody that he had a friend who had a collection of bugs bigger than his hand and a jar filled with real live African lion poop.

**A NORMAL-SIZE HAND BUT NOT
A NORMAL-SIZE BUG**

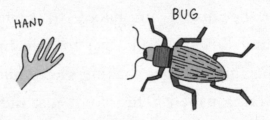

Of course no one was believing him. No one except me. Though I didn't think he was being completely full of truthfulness by calling Mrs. Luther his friend. For sure they didn't share sips from the same cup, give each other cheer-up hugs, or swear to keep real important things secret, which are all things that are done by a real 100 percent for real friend.

But I didn't say anything because I didn't want anyone and mostly him to think that I was taking his side. Sammy Stringer and I are not and will never be friends! Mimi said she was glad her dad bought his paper at the train station so they didn't have to have a paperboy. I told her I wished I could say that too.

Liar, Liar I Wish Your Pants Were On Fire

Grace F. was her usual Big Meanie self today and was trying to make up as many reasons as she could to call me Just Grace in front of every person in the entire class. When Miss Lois asked her about the capital city of Wisconsin she said, "Oh, I can't remember, but I think Just Grace has a cousin that lives there." This was totally untrue and just a big lie, because I don't have any cousins, and even if I did I would never tell Grace F. one single thing about them, especially where they lived.

So before she could say another made-up thing about me I said, "She's lying! I do not have any cousins in that state or even in the entire world."

Miss Lois gave me one of her concentration looks and said, "Just Grace, you know better than to speak out without raising your hand. Do you know what city is the capital of Wisconsin?" Of course I could not think of the right answer to that question, plus,

Wisconsin is such a hard name to remember all by itself. When I thought about it, it filled up my brain and there was not even enough room left for a probably impossible-to-remember city name as well. Miss Lois was still staring at me and I couldn't think of anything to say that she would like to hear. Miss Lois looked back and forth at me and the Big Meanie, and then she said, "Well, girls, as homework you two can do some research on Wisconsin, and when you come back on Monday you can tell the class two interesting facts about the state as well as the name of the capital city."

"Are we doing it together?" The Big Meanie gave me a if-I-have-to-work-with-you-I-will-throw-up look.

"Sure, if you girls want to work together you can," said Miss Lois. This time I put my hand up. "I don't want to, *thank you,*" I said, and I mean-looked right back at Grace F.! Instead of "thank you" what I wanted to say was "even if I were almost the last person in the whole world and all my friends were dead and Grace F. were the only person I would get to talk with for a whole month, or even a year, I still would 100 percent not want to work with her!" But you can't say stuff like that in a class in front of a teacher and not get in trouble.

Miss Lois shook her head like she does when she seems confused and does not understand what is going on. She probably thinks that all the Graces should be friends. She does not get that some Graces are nicer and better than other Graces.

When I looked behind me I could see that Sammy Stringer was looking right at me and smiling, with something gross stuck on his front tooth. I hoped that it was on purpose, because I don't know why, but something stuck on your tooth by accident seems a lot grosser.

The Completely Surprising Thing Happens Again

After school I saw Sammy Stringer get invited into Mrs. Luther's house again. I am not spying on Mrs. Luther and definitely not spying on Sammy Stringer, but every time I look out the window I just see them. I can understand why Sammy Stringer would think that Mrs. Luther is cool—she has that lion poop collection, which is probably making him crazy with excited joy. He just loves poop.

But the reason Mrs. Luther would like him is harder to figure out. She could just be super, super, super, super lonely or else she could be doing one of those anthropology studies on Sammy. The kind where she studies strange people that live in countries that no one has ever heard of before. Only Sammy lives here, but he is so strange so maybe that part doesn't matter.

And Then...

I tried to draw a Not So adventure so that I wouldn't use all my concen-

MRS. LUTHER STUDYING SAMMY.
SHE IS WRITING THINGS DOWN.

tration on Mrs. Luther and Sammy Stringer, but I couldn't do it.

Sometimes it's not very easy to stop yourself from thinking of something once your brain has started thinking about that thing. I drew Sammy Stringer and Mrs. Luther even though they were the exact things I was trying not to think about.

If You Hear Some Strange Noises Out Your Window You Should Probably Look And See What It Is

Mrs. Luther was standing on her porch, shouting at Sammy. At first I thought she was mad at him, which wasn't so hard to imagine to be true, but then I could tell that she was yelling directions. "Run to the left. Now go straight. No, wait, quick—run to the right."

Sammy was wearing two big red oven mitts over his hands and was flapping his arms up and down, over and over again. He was running like crazy all over Mrs. Luther's yard, just like one of those giant ostriches they have at the zoo. At the zoo you have to be careful and not get too close or they'll peck you in the eye. Ostriches like shiny things like coins and eyeballs. Mrs. Luther might have put a spell on him and changed his brain to think he was an ostrich. Sometimes if something is bad for the person who it is happening to it can still be funny if you are the one watching and it is not you running around like a big crazy bird.

OSTRICH   BOY

But it was maybe not so funny if Sammy Stringer was going to think he was an ostrich forever. That would be bad, even for someone I did not like. Then when I saw Crinkles run under a bush, I knew what was the truth. Sammy Stringer was trying to catch Crinkles. Why he was doing it with big red oven mitts must have been a secret cat-catching reason. If Crinkles didn't like Mrs. Luther's orange cast, it didn't seem that he would be happy to be grabbed by big flapping red oven mitties.

"Go left! He's right there on your left!" shouted Mrs. Luther. She was waving her arms and jumping up and down at the top of her steps, which is maybe something you should not do with a big orange cast on your leg. Crinkles ran right past Sammy, through the fence and into our yard. I could tell he was going to exactly the place where he was not supposed to go. I was right about the cast and jumping, because the next time I looked at the steps Mrs. Luther was lying on them and Sammy was trying to help her up. She stood up and shooed Sammy's help away.

All the fun was over. Crinkles was gone, Mrs. Luther was limping like normal, and Sammy was not being Ostrich Boy. I ran downstairs and found Crinkles just where I knew he would be. I would make a good cat detective. Crinkles was sitting on Augustine Dupre's table, drinking milk from one of her very fancy French teacups—the ones that always make me feel special and nervous to touch because they look like they could break into a million pieces really easy.

"Crinkles is very upset. He jumped in the window and wouldn't stop meowing, so I gave him some milk to calm him down. I think his fear of Mrs. Luther is getting worse," said Augustine Dupre. "I am getting very worried." She petted Crinkles behind his ears. Crinkles did not look upset at all. He looked very happy.

I told her all about Sammy, Mrs. Luther, and the big red oven mitts. "This is very strange, very strange indeed," said Augustine Dupre, and she picked up Crinkles and held him close. She didn't say anything else, but it seemed like maybe Augustine Dupre was in love with Crinkles too!

The Bad Thing Augustine Dupre Told Me

Augustine Dupre told me she had to leave the next day on an emergency trip to France, and that it could not be helped, but the sad truth was she would be gone for two whole weeks. She would not be around to help with any part of my big idea! Not the taking-the-photo-of-Crinkles part, not the blowing-up-the-picture part, and not the gluing part. Nothing!

I tried to talk to her about what to do next, but she was not being a good listener like she normally is. She was putting all her clothes into little piles and doing lots of French sighing that had nothing to do with me or Crinkles. Crinkles went and sat right in the middle of Augustine Dupre's suitcase, like he was hoping that she was going to take him to France with her, but she said she would not do a thing like that even though she would miss him.

I could tell Crinkles was hoping that she was lying to me. He wanted to go anywhere Augustine Dupre was going to go. He was in love.

Taking The Photo Of Crinkles

Today was a beautiful sunny day. It was perfect outside weather to take a picture of Crinkles, and that was too bad because Augustine Dupre, my big helper, was gone. When you are going to France you have to get up and leave really early in the morning.

After breakfast, which was not French toast because Mom said she was tired of it and so we had to have pancakes instead, I went outside to find Crinkles. He was walking around in our front yard. I was happy to see that he was not on his way to France with Augustine Dupre, but I was not happy about how he was not being at all helpful with my project.

No matter how hard I tried and tried, and talked to him in a nice, not mad voice, he was still not a good photo subject. Every time I put him in a perfect sit-up pose, the second I stepped back to take the photo he'd lie down and roll all over the ground the way he does when he wants to be petted. He would not stay sitting up. And then even after I petted him for maybe ten minutes, he still wanted more pets. I cannot believe that he is that lonely and misses Augustine Dupre already. He is a very needy cat. This is the kind of thing you say when you are talking about someone who takes up all your energy and never seems full.

Finally, I just had to wait for him to stand up and then take his picture when he was walking. It was not excellent, but he still looked nice with the sun shining on his fur. He is a very nice-looking cat. In photography language, someone who looks good in photos gets to be called photogenic. Crinkles is photogenic.

THE POSE I WANTED **THE POSE I GOT**

Mom drove me to the photocopy store.

If she thinks I am doing a project for school she is always happy to help. I didn't say my project was not for school and she didn't ask if my project was for school, so we both were thinking different things were the truth. When this kind of thing happens it is called a miscommunication. It is not a lie, and this is good because I am not a liar.

Mom doesn't like to stand around inside the copy store, so she took a magazine and waited in the car, which was good for me, because she would for sure want to know why I needed a cat-size picture of Crinkles if she saw it. She would not understand my project.

The lady in the store was helpful about blowing up the Crinkles photo. Her name was Chuck, which is usually a boy's name, but that is what her nametag on her apron said. Chuck said that Crinkles looked like a very nice cat and I said he was, but I did not tell her more because I did not want one more lady to fall in love with him. I got two big pictures of Crinkles in case I made a mistake, because the cutting and gluing is always hard to do right.

CARDBOARD CRINKLES

Looking at cardboard Crinkles made me smile. I couldn't wait for Mimi to come over and see him. She would love him like she could never love a real cat, and that would be a great thing for her.

Tomorrow we were going to make a plan about where to take the pictures. Mimi said she would be happy to help make cardboard Crinkles stand up in all sorts of places. It was something I was so excited about that I could hardly go to sleep. Cardboard Crinkles slept in my closet, and I could not believe how real he looked every time I opened the door to check on him. Everything was going to work out just perfect, I could tell.

What I Learned About Wisconsin Before Mimi Came Over

I had to do my Wisconsin homework before Mimi came over. That is what Mom said, and then she said she was going to check it, which means I had to do a good job and not just write down some stuff real hasty, which is her favorite word for meaning not taking time to do something properly.

My first fact was about the National Freshwater Fishing Hall of Fame. A fishing museum does not sound very exciting, except for the special fact that outside the museum is a supersize giant fish that you can climb up into. You can even stand in its mouth and wave at the people down on the ground in the parking lot. It is the world's biggest not real muskie, which is good because if it was a real fish it would probably be the biggest monster fish in the lake.

ME WAVING FROM INSIDE A MUSKIE

HIGH IN
THE AIR

My second fact about Wisconsin was the circus parade, which happens right through the middle of a city called Milwaukee. At the end of the parade the circus people give out rides on the elephants, camels, and zebras. I don't know if this can be true, because I have never seen a person ride a zebra, but I hope that it is real, because a zebra ride sounds very fun and like something I would be happy to have a photo of.

ME WAVING ON THE BACK OF A ZEBRA

Some other facts about Wisconsin are the state insect, which is the honeybee, and the invention of the first ice cream sundae in a city called Two Rivers. These are not as exciting as my first two facts, which I am hoping that Grace F. does not pick. I will be mad if she gets to go first and she chooses the same two interesting facts about Wisconsin as I have, and then tells about them like they are hers.

Mimi Is In Love

Mimi never gets to go near real cats, so she was super excited to hold Crinkles. I took a picture of her with him and in the camera it looked like she was holding a real cat. She said she was in love with cardboard Crinkles, which was okay because it was not the real Crinkles, who already had too much love in his cat life.

After we made a map and a plan, because it is always good to know what you are doing so mistakes will not happen, Mimi and cardboard Crinkles and I went outside to take the photos. We did not see the real Crinkles, for which Mimi was glad.

MAP OF WHERE TO TAKE THE
PHOTOS OF CRINKLES

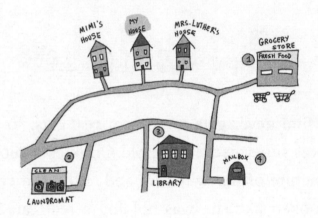

Cardboard Crinkles was a great photo subject—he stood still and never looked away or flopped down when he was supposed to be standing up. When we took the picture of Crinkles in the shopping cart at the grocery store, a man came by and asked about our cat. He thought cardboard Crinkles was real! Mimi was so excited, she couldn't stop jumping up and down.

We couldn't wait to get home and get the pictures out of the camera to make the postcards. Dad has shown me how to do this with the computer, and it is pretty easy if you don't press any of the wrong keys on the keyboard. Usually I am allowed to use the computer only when Dad is there to help, but I knew just what to do already, so it was okay. The computer always asks you lots of questions, and as long as you don't say yes when it asks you about the word *delete,* things will not go really bad. Really bad is when Dad uses lots of grown-up words that I am not allowed to say, and then he has to talk for forever on the phone to a computer person who tries to help him fix what is wrong. This makes Dad very grumpy, mad, and not a fun dad. I did not want this to happen.

POSTCARD NUMBER ONE

Hi! I was thinking of you and how you love going to the grocery store! Maybe I could come with you sometime!
Love,
Crinkles

Mrs. Luther
782 Marshfield Lane
Morgan, N.J.

Writing the postcard was not very easy, and not as fast as we thought it would be. There was a lot of hard stuff to figure out right at the start of the postcard. "Dear Mrs. Luther" sounded too official-like, and we decided that "Human Mommy" sounded too weird—like maybe Crinkles was an alien or something. That's why we had to just write "Hi." It was the only thing that would work.

After that we had to decide why Crinkles would want to send a postcard from the grocery store in the first place. Projects sure get a lot more complicated once you are really doing them and not just thinking about doing them.

Writing postcard number two was easier because most of the hard stuff was already figured out from doing postcard number

Hi again! So this is
where you take my
favorite cozy blanket to
be washed. I miss not
being cozy with you.
 Love,
 Crinkles

Mrs. Luther
782 Marshfield Lane
Morgan, N.J.

one. Mimi did the writing on the postcard just in case Mrs. Luther would recognize my handwriting style since I lived right next door to her.

Mimi wanted to write all the postcards at once, but I said this would not be a good idea, because then it would be too hard to not mail them all right away. When something is super fun, it is hard to make yourself stop doing that something, even if you say, "We should not do this super-fun thing anymore." And then what would happen is that Mrs. Luther would get all her postcards on the same day, which was not the way the big idea was supposed to go. Mimi made me promise that we could make some more postcards tomorrow. And she made me promise that I would not put any more in the mailbox if she was not with me.

These were not hard promises to make, because Mimi is my best friend and it is always more fun to do stuff with her than to do stuff by myself. I could hardly keep my joy inside me, I was so excited. We ran to the mailbox and mailed postcard number one. I couldn't wait for Mrs. Luther to get it and start feeling better right away. This is my favorite part of being a sort-of superhero.

Wisconsin And Lion Poop

Grace F. did not get to go first about telling two interesting facts about Wisconsin. This was like a big present for me. Miss Lois said she was very impressed about my Wisconsin discoveries and said that an elephant ride sounded like an exciting thing to try. This was kind of a surprise, since I could not even imagine Miss Lois riding on a bicycle, which is a more normal thing to ride than an elephant.

Grace F. seemed really mad when it was her turn and said that her number one interesting fact about Wisconsin was the giant muskie, but that since I had already used it up she didn't want to talk about it again. I said, "Well, you can tell about the honeybee or the ice cream sundae. I didn't use those ones."

"Just Grace! What have I told you about speaking out of turn without raising your hand!" Miss Lois was mad at me.

"She's ruined it! Now I don't have one single thing to tell about Wisconsin! She told everything!" Grace F. was mad too. She was pointing at me, and she was talking, and she was not raising her hand.

Miss Lois was shaking her head again. "Okay, girls. Let's just all calm down." Then

WASP

MEAN

she made Grace F. tell us her two facts even though I had already told about them. When she said the honeybee was the insect of Wisconsin, she did not say that honeybees and wasps are not the same thing and that it can be con-

fusing to tell the difference. This is something I would have said, but I was not going to help her with her part of the project anymore.

HONEYBEE

FRIENDLY

Sammy brought lion poop in a glass jar for his show and tell for animal week. Most people bring books about animals or a photo of their favorite pet. I am certain that no one in the entire class has ever brought real poop to school before. Everybody except me was impressed. What is so great about lion poop? Even Miss Lois seemed impressed, which was the second surprise I had about her in one day.

Sammy looked over and smiled at me. I did not smile back. I did not want him to think that I shared his joy about animal poop, which I certainly do not. Olivia Berchelli brought in a picture of her cat, Pookie. Sammy Stringer put his hand up and said, "I don't like cats." This was a not nice thing to say and also a very strange thing to say, since a lion is really just a very big cat. It is hard for me to think nice things about him. He is too much hard work.

Spying For A Good Reason Is Not Bad

As soon as I got home from school I ran up to my room to look out my window. I was hoping I would see Mrs. Luther smiling and holding up my postcard, but instead I saw nothing. Her drapes were closed! This was very mysterious and confusing. She had never closed the drapes before. What was she doing in there? A dance of joy or a dance of sadness and crying? I couldn't decide what to think.

Augustine Dupre was not around to talk to, and I did not feel like drawing a comic, and I could not watch TV because it was before dinnertime, so I went outside for a walk around the house. Maybe Mrs. Luther was outside too. She was not. Even Crinkles was not.

Walking around the house is not a very interesting thing to do if you do it more than three times in a row. I closed Augustine Dupre's window, which she had left open by mistake, and went back inside.

WALKING AROUND HOUSE

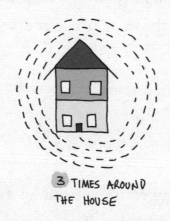

3 TIMES AROUND THE HOUSE

I called Mimi and told her we had to have an emergency mailing and mail postcard number two right away. She couldn't come over, so I had to go do it by myself. It was not as much fun as mailing postcard number one. Then there was nothing more to do. Just wait. Waiting is not fun no matter where you are. It is always mostly boring and long, even if you try to find something to do.

After dinner we all watched a new episode of *Unlikely Heroes*. Mom is right! It is a feel-good show. It made me feel so much better.

Trouble

Sammy Stringer is in trouble. He took the glass jar with the lion poop from Mrs. Luther's house without asking her permission. This is stealing, but Sammy said he was just borrowing it, which is probably true but

still bad if you do it without asking.

The principal made
Sammy go and give it back
to Mrs. Luther, and then
he had to apologize to her.
The worst thing about this

LION POOP IN JAR

is that he had to do it in front of her class,
which was filled up with all the big kids.
Some of them were being mean and laughing until Mrs. Luther made them all be quiet.
This is probably what made Sammy cry, all
the big kids being quiet and watching him. It
is really hard to say you're sorry when you
are trying to stop your eyes from crying in
front of lots of people you don't know. Poor
Sammy.

After the whole thing happened he had
to go to the nurse's office for a while to calm
himself down and try to make his face not

look like it had been crying. He is going to know that we all know he cried, even if we pretend we don't know a thing about it. It is going to be hard for him to walk around and pretend everything is normal when it most certainly is not. I was feeling sad for him. I couldn't help it. When he came back to our class I turned around, and when he looked at me I smiled. This was probably a bad idea, but I had to do it.

More Postcards

After school Mimi came over and we glued two more postcards together. Writing the message on the back is the most fun part. We signed these ones with a big heart next to the pawprint so that Mrs. Luther would know

POSTCARD NUMBER THREE

There are so many really good books about cats here. Did you ever know that one of my favorite things is books about cats? One of my other favorite things is you!

Love,
Crinkles

Mrs. Luther
782 Marshfield Lane
Morgan, N.J.

POSTCARD NUMBER FOUR

This is how I send my
postcards to you. I hope
you like them.
    I miss you!

    Love,
    Crinkles

Mrs. Luther
782 Marshfield Lane
Morgan, N.J.

that Crinkles loved her. Even though I am a little bit mad at Mrs. Luther for making Sammy cry in front of the big kids, we still mailed postcard number three. She probably didn't know he was going to cry, so maybe it wasn't so much her fault.

Mimi wanted me to take more photos of her with Crinkles, but I had an even better idea—I told her she could have the extra cardboard Crinkles to take home. She was so happy, she hugged and hugged me until I had to tell her to stop, because it was not feeling so nice to be hugged so much. Too many hugs is not a good thing. It is too bad that she has her allergy. I can just tell that she would love real cats if she could get close to them. I am extra lucky that way.

It Was A Bad Idea

Smiling at Sammy Stringer yesterday was a bad idea. Today he was smiling back at me every single time I just-by-accident looked at him. He probably thinks I like him and that we are going to be friends. All because I gave him a teeny tiny I-feel-sorry-for-you smile yesterday. If he thinks we will have lunch together and pick each other as partners in gym class, he is totally wrong. I would never give up Jordan, who is my best gym friend, and even if she went on vacation to Hawaii, like she is going to do in two months, I would still not pick Sammy Stringer as my gym partner. I would for sure pick someone else instead.

Sammy's smile-at-me would not go

away! It smiled at me for the whole entire school day! I could not get rid of it no matter how hard I tried, and even after I mean-looked at him, it was still there. I was glad to go home!

Spying Is Hard

After school I saw Mrs. Luther on her front porch. She was carrying lots and lots of papers, so I couldn't tell if some of them were my postcards. I also couldn't tell if she looked happy. She was having a lot of trouble holding on to all her stuff while she was try-ing to open her front door. It's probably not good to watch someone have trouble and not do anything about it, but I didn't want her to know I was spying on her. I wish she would open her drapes so I could see if she looks happy when she is inside her house.

I went outside and walked to the mailbox on the corner to mail postcard number four. Mimi said it would be okay if I did it by myself. If this one doesn't work I don't know what else we can do.

There was no one outside anywhere. I didn't even see Crinkles. He might be hiding and sad because Augustine Dupre is in France. I am starting to get sad about that too. I thought that Crinkles and I could maybe be sad about that together, but he is not around, so we will both have to be sad alone instead. This project is not working as perfectly as I thought it would. I made some Not So Super comic drawings in my notebook, but it did not cheer me up even one little bit.

SUPERHERO IDEAS

Trouble Times Two

Sammy is in trouble again. He got called into the principal's office right in the middle of reading class, which is a very unusual thing to happen. Jordan was in the nurse's office right next door. She tripped while she was running and hurt her ankle, so she got to miss reading class. It is much more fun to read in the nurse's office because the nurse has lots of magazines to look at and for some reason Miss Lois says, "Magazines are not the same as books and they don't count for reading," so we don't get to have them in our classroom.

BOOK VERSUS MAGAZINE

WORDS AND MAYBE SOME PICTURES

PHOTOGRAPHS, WORDS, AND PICTURES

Jordan told Mimi and me all about Sammy's trouble when she came back from the nurse's office at lunchtime. Jordan said the principal was in the office with Mrs. Luther and she got to hear everything they said to Sammy, but she could not understand what Sammy said back because he was crying and it was too hard to understand him.

What they are thinking is so crazy that I cannot believe they would think such a thing could be true. They think that Sammy catnapped Crinkles to be mean to Mrs. Luther because she got mad at him for stealing the lion poop. Mrs. Luther said that Crinkles has been missing for two days and it is not like him to not come home to eat, even if he is scared of her orange cast. When they said, "Revenge is a serious crime," Sammy started crying so hard, they had to make him breathe into a paper bag so he wouldn't choke and die. After that they called his mom to come to the school and get him.

BREATHE IN AND OUT IN THE PAPER BAG. IT HELPS CALM YOU DOWN.

"I knew that Sammy Stringer was no good!" said Mimi.

"He's disgusting and mean!" said Jordan.

"That's true," I said. "But he doesn't like cats." I remembered in my imagination him flapping around Mrs. Luther's yard with the big red oven mitts over his hands.

"Exactly," said Jordan. "He's a catnapper!"

"Poor Crinkles," said Mimi, and she looked like she was going to cry.

"No! He doesn't like cats because he's scared of them! He's a scaredy-cat. But scared of cats! He wouldn't hurt Crinkles. He's probably even too chicken to touch him." I was just like one of those super-smart detectives on Mom's TV crime show. They always put their hands on their hips when they have finished solving a very

tricky crime, so I did it too. "Ta-da!" I said. "He is innocent!"

"Ta-da," said Jordan, "he is not! They have proof! Sammy sent Mrs. Luther ransom notes that had cat photos on them and everything. He even made her cat sit in a grocery cart. So see? He had to touch it!"

Trouble For Me

It is no fun getting in trouble, and it is very much no fun knowing that you are going to be in trouble, even if the trouble part hasn't happened yet. Mimi and I didn't know what we were going to do. I knew that Mimi didn't catnap Crinkles and she knew that I didn't catnap Crinkles, but we knew that it was us that had sent the ransom notes, only they weren't ransom notes but feel-good postcards. And right now they were not making me or her feel very good.

I wasn't feeling so bad for Sammy Stringer anymore—I was feeling more bad for me! He was going to be fine. He probably hadn't done any more wrong things at all.

I wished some kind of empathy superhero could come along to save me. I wanted it really bad, but even if you close your eyes and wish real hard for superhero help, nothing is going to happen, so I kept my eyes open.

And then, because we had to, because we are good people, Mimi and I went to the principal's office by ourselves, on purpose, and told Mr. Harris, our principal, everything.

After we finished our explaining of the big idea, Mr. Harris was not as mad as we thought he was going to be. I was feeling good that I did not cry and that Mimi did not cry. Crying is something that sometimes happens even if you don't want it to. It is hard to keep control of it and make it not happen.

Mr. Harris said he was glad that we had been filled up with lots of "good intentions." These are the I'm-sure-this-is-the-perfect-thing-to-do feelings you have right before you do something to help someone else. Real superheroes must have a lot of these.

Mrs. Luther was not as glad about the "good intentions" as Mr. Harris was. She looked at us like we were maybe not 100 percent telling her the truth. She said it was troubling and strange how Crinkles disappeared right when we started sending her the postcards.

We nodded our heads to say, "Yes, you are right, that is very strange and very troubling," but that didn't make her any happier. The way Mrs. Luther was being made me think that maybe she was not the kind of person who deserved the feel-good postcards in the first place. She was making me have bad feelings about my empathy superhero powers, which is not a good thing to feel.

Then Mrs. Luther surprised us and said, "I'm relieved none of this had anything to do with Sammy Stringer. He really is quite an interesting boy, very curious. I must apologize to him."

BEFORE APOLOGY   AFTER APOLOGY

Grownups hardly ever say they are sorry to kids, and I don't think I have ever heard of a teacher doing an apology to a student before. Mrs. Luther gave us one more look and then walked away to go say she was sorry to Sammy Stringer. He was going to be shocked and surprised!

Mimi was right. The helper does not get in as much trouble as the number one planner.

Mr. Harris said he had to call my dad to explain everything, not because he wanted to get me in trouble but just because parents had a right to know certain things and this was one of those certain things. And I knew that it was exactly the kind of certain thing that Dad and Mom would not understand and do lots of loud talking about, which would end up with me getting in trouble.

Mr. Harris didn't call Mimi's dad. He said that dad could drop Mimi off at her house on our way home.

Thing I DiD Not Get In Trouble For

Wanting to help someone else. Dad said this is an important thing, but not so important that it makes all the other things I did get in trouble for disappear right out of his memory. This is too bad, because if that happened I would not be getting in trouble and would maybe be getting a medal or something instead.

Things I Got In Trouble For

1 Making Mom take me to the copy store for a project that was not for school.

This was not really fair, since it is impossible to make Mom do anything she does not want to do, but when I said this Mom said, "Do not press your luck, young lady!" and then I didn't say anything more because when Mom calls me "young lady" she is really mad. This I know from when it has happened before.

NAMES MOM CALLS ME WHEN SHE IS ANGRY

YOUNG LADY!
GRACE STEWART!
MISSY!

2 Using the computer and the expensive photo paper without asking Dad.

Dad did not act really really mad about this, and I could tell that he was maybe a little bit proud that I had done so much computer work all by myself without anything going wrong. Mom was standing right next to him so he had to pretend to be mad, and she did not see him wink at me.

3 Walking all over the neighborhood without telling Mom and Dad where I was going.

This was the biggest get-in-trouble of all, and when they were saying it I wished I were invisible and could sneak away so I wouldn't have to hear how worried sick they said they would have been if they had known what I was doing, even though it was over and I was standing right in front of them, 100 percent perfectly fine. Making your parents worried sick is not a good feeling.

4 Dad said all the other things in one sentence, so that means that they were small troubles and nothing he was going to remember forever and ever until I was all grown up, like the other stuff. These things were taking the stamps without asking, spying on Mrs. Luther, and being a bad example to Mimi. I know that Mimi does not need me to help her be a bad example, but I did not say that right then because it was not a good way to get the trouble-talk to stop.

STAMPS TALKING

The almost worst part about the whole getting-in-trouble was that Dad said I had to walk over to Mrs. Luther's house and apologize for the postcards all over again, even though I already said I was sorry to her at school. Dad even came with me to make sure I did it right.

I was hoping and hoping that Mrs.

MRS. LUTHER'S WITCH DRESS

Luther would not be home, but I was not lucky about that, because she answered the door in her rainbow witch dress. I said, "I'm really sorry about the postcards." And then Mrs. Luther said, "That's all right, dear. I suppose it's quite flattering that you went to so much trouble, isn't it?" Which was something I did not understand but I nodded "yes" because yes is mostly the right answer if you are confused by a grownup's question and the grownup is smiling when she asks you. If she is not smiling, then the answer is probably no.

Then Mrs. Luther asked Dad if he had seen the postcards, and when he said no she went to get them. I asked Dad if I could go home, because I was standing there 100 percent sure that seeing the postcards was going to make him all mad again. He said, "You are not to move," which means, "No, you cannot go home," but it does not mean I have to be perfectly like a statue still.

Dad Is Not So Mad

Dad and Mrs. Luther talked, and talked, and talked about the postcards and how wonderful they looked. Dad said he could not believe that it was not Crinkles standing in the shopping cart. I was trying not to smile, so I looked at the ground and Mrs. Luther's scary masks behind her. Not smiling is hard to do, but when you are in trouble it is better to stay looking sad so you won't have to get told again about how much trouble you are in. When you are in trouble, looking sad and unhappy for a pretty long time makes your parents think you are very, very, sorry.

On the way home Dad said, "I'm very impressed with you, but that does not mean you are not in trouble and grounded for one week."

Revenge

Mrs. Luther is not friendly! Yesterday she was only pretending to be nice, because last night I am 100 percent sure that she sent some ghosts over to my house to punish me. I heard them when it was dark and I was sleeping. They were making scary spooky sounds right near my room!

SLEEPING CHAIR

Mom and Dad let me sleep in their room on the big chair in the corner. I think Mom whispered to Dad that she heard something too, but she didn't make him put on his clothes to go outside and look around.

In the morning Dad looked in my room

and outside my window but he couldn't find anything creepy or scary. The only thing he found was Sammy Stringer, who was poking around in our yard. Dad invited Sammy to come inside our house, which I could not believe! And it was right when I was eating breakfast, so Dad asked him if he wanted some pancakes too. I had to sit across from the disgusting Sammy Stringer and watch him eat food, at my very own breakfast table!

Dad said, "Your friend Sammy here was outside looking for Mrs. Luther's cat. Maybe after breakfast you'd like to give him a hand? You seem to know all about that cat. It'd be nice to get that poor woman back her pet."

Mom came downstairs and gave Sammy and me one of her super-big surprised looks. I was mad at Sammy Stringer for getting invited into my very own house and eating my very own pancakes right in front of me, so I said, "How come you're not wearing your red oven mitts?"

HOW SAMMY SHOULD EAT PANCAKES

SAMMY EATING PANCAKES
WITH OVEN MITTS.
HA! HA!

I was not going to be nice, even if I did save him from trouble because I couldn't help but do it, and even if he was in my house.

"I'm not going to touch the cat, I'm just going to find him. Mrs. Luther said if I could find him she would let me have that jar of lion poop for my collection and I could keep it forever."

"Well, that's certainly a prize!" said Mom. I don't know how she could smile so nice and not make a disgusted face like I did —she is really good at pretend faces.

"I'll tell you what," said Dad, pointing at me. "You two do a team-up and find that cat and I'll forget about the grounding. Deal?"

"Deal!" said Sammy even though it was not his deal, because Dad was not even talking to him. He was talking to me.

"Great," said Dad. And Sammy Stringer smiled at me with his mouth sort of open, so I could see all the bits of pancakes in between his teeth.

Forced Partner

Sammy wanted to do lots of talking and acting like we were friends on a special cat-finding mission, but I told him right away the truth.

I said, "Sammy Stringer, I am not going to be your friend. I am only doing this cat project with you because my dad says I have to."

"Me too!" said Sammy, but then he wouldn't be quiet and kept asking me all about how I made the postcards, and if I was going to make any more. I don't think he has very good understanding skills!

We looked all over Mrs. Luther's yard and all over my yard, and even in Mimi's yard, which did not make me happy, because I did not want Mimi to see me with Sammy Stringer, even if I was not talking and being friends with him. We looked and looked and looked, but we did not find Crinkles.

I broke my don't-talk-to-Sammy rule and said, "I guess Crinkles ran away. Mrs. Luther is just too scary for him to be around."

"She's not scary," said Sammy, and he was looking at me like he could not understand what I was saying. "She's really cool and interesting, plus, she makes the best cookies ever because they have . . . Hey! What's that sound?"

It was the ghosts—they were back and still scary-sounding, even in the daytime.

"It's ghosts! She sent them over here

**WHAT THE GHOSTS PROBABLY
LOOK LIKE**

to scare me!" My insides were shaking and I was pulling at Sammy's jacket, which I would not do if things were normal because I would never in a million years touch him on purpose.

"She's mad because of the postcards. Come on! Let's get my dad!" But Sammy was not moving.

"She's not mad. She's got the postcards on her fridge—she likes them. What, do you think she's a witch or something?" Sammy walked away from me and then I heard him yell! I couldn't understand what he was saying. My brain said, "Save Sammy or run for help?" I was running for help when he yelled again, and this time I heard him. He was yelling, "It's Crinkles!"

Crinkles

I ran around the corner of my house, right into Sammy's pointing finger. It was pointing right at me and he said, "You were the cat-napper all along! You're a liar!!" Then he pointed at Augustine Dupre's window, which is on my house. Crinkles was looking out at us from inside, and he was making the horrible ghost noises.

~~Forced~~ Partner

It took a long time to tell Sammy Stringer the truth of why Crinkles would be in my house by accident. A normal person would understand the reason really fast, but Sammy Stinger is not a normal person. Plus, he asked me a million hundred questions about every little thing, so the whole story took forever! At the end he believed me that I was not an on-purpose catnapper, which was good, because I was not in a hurry to get into even more trouble. We both looked at Crinkles and we each had our own thoughts, because we did not say anything. My thoughts were . . .

1   I cannot let Dad know where Crinkles is.

2 I must get Crinkles out of Augustine Dupre's apartment.

3 I only want to be grounded for a week ... not longer, even if things go really, really bad.

I do not know what Sammy Stringer's thoughts were, but I bet they were not as many or as hard as mine.

I had to trade promises with Sammy Stringer so that we could both, in the end, get the thing we wanted. It made us real partners instead of pretend partners like before, which was not so perfect if I thought about who I was a partner with, but much better than being alone if I thought about what I had to do next—it is not easy to be sneaky and careful at the same time if you are all alone.

I tried to open the window, but the little latch thing had snapped closed and the window would not open even a sliver. Sammy said he would stay by the window and talk nice to Crinkles to keep him from howling while I did the sneaking-upstairs part to borrow the spare apartment key from Dad's desk. Sammy also had the job of keeping everyone away from the window in case someone was nosy and came too close. I was not sure if he could do these two things at the same time, but I had to trust him.

Finding the exact key was not easy, because Dad keeps his entire key collection all together in one box and none of the keys has any writing on it to say what it is for. I had to take the whole box outside to Augustine Dupre's door and try almost every single one in the door.

Sammy was nervous that Crinkles would jump through the door the minute I put the right key in, like he was an attack lion or something. If I liked talking to him I would have said, "Don't you think it's crazy to be scared of a cat when you think lions are so great?" but I didn't say that. I said, "He won't jump out. He's just a furry little cozy kittie."

I don't know if Sammy could tell, but

what I said was a little bit mean, but then, because I am not good at being mean, even if someone sort of deserves it like he does, I gave him the two oven mitts I brought down from upstairs so he could protect himself. Sammy seemed a lot happier even though he looked completely silly.

Crinkles was crazy with joy when I opened the door. I told Sammy to stand guard outside until I locked Crinkles in the bathroom, which was not so easy to do because he kept sneaking out when I tried to push him in—plus, his claws were sharp and pointy.

Finally Crinkles was locked up so I could let Sammy in. "It stinks in here! Like a cat bathroom!" said Sammy. He made a really good disgusted face and was trying to hold his nose closed with the big oven mitties.

He was right! It smelled terrible! This whole time while he was locked in, Crinkles was using Augustine Dupre's two fancy trees in pots as a cat toilet.

"Yuck! It's disgusting! It's coming from there," I said, and I pointed at the plants. I 100 percent did not want to touch the smelly pots filled with Crinkles's cat poop, even though I liked Crinkles and he is a very nice cat.

"I'll do it. I'll take them outside," said Sammy. "It's fair, because you have to do the carry-the-cat part." And then right there, even though I could hardly believe it, Sammy turned into the exact perfect-for-me partner. I hate poop and I love cats, and he hates cats and he loves poop. The chance of this per-

fect-partner-happening was probably something like .008 percent.

While Sammy was outside I looked for
some kind of perfumey stuff to spray around
the apartment. Augustine Dupre is fancy, so
she had lots of choices. I used a little bit of
each one, and pretty soon I couldn't even tell
if the cat smell was there anymore.

Sammy said he wanted to wait outside
the apartment when I went upstairs to take
back the keys and the oven mitts. I don't
think he wanted to be in the apartment alone
with Crinkles, but he said it was because he
didn't like the smell of the fancy perfumes.

Cat Return

Sammy walked in front of me and Crinkles just in case Crinkles got away. If Crinkles escaped me, which he was not going to do because I know how to hold a cat, Sammy thought Crinkles would run back to my house instead of in front to Mrs. Luther's house, and he did not want to be a person who was in Crinkles's way. This was perfect with me, because I did not want to be the first person Mrs. Luther saw when she opened her front door.

This was not a problem, because even though Sammy was standing in front, the first thing Mrs. Luther saw was Crinkles. She told me to hold him tight and come in quick so she could close the door so he couldn't run off. Then she asked us to go into the scary mask room and sit down.

I gave her Crinkles and he sat on Mrs. Luther's lap, giving her leg a massage with his claws. This is something cats do when they are happy, and she didn't seem to mind that his claws were sharp and pointy. Mrs. Luther wiped some probably happy tears away from her eyes and said, "So where did you find him?"

I could not believe that Sammy and I had forgotten all about practicing this part.

"Under some bushes near Grace's house."

Yeah, Sammy! He remembered his promise, and he didn't even call me Just Grace like normal.

"Well, thank you, Grace, and thank you, Sammy, for everything." And then Mrs. Luther winked at me and her smile didn't look exactly so much like a crocodile's.

"Sammy, run into the kitchen and get some cookies for you and your friend. He loves my cookies, that Sammy," said Mrs. Luther, and she smiled again—definitely not crocodile-like this time either.

Sammy was right. Mrs. Luther's cookies were amazing. They had real pieces of chocolate bar right in the cookies, which was such a great idea and one I had never seen or eaten before. The masks on the wall still looked kind of scary even up close, but they did not look scarier than they did from my room, which was not how I thought it was going to be. And there was my room, right through Mrs. Luther's window. She could see

COOKIES

REAL CHOCOLATE BARS

me as well as I could see her. This was not something I had thought about either.

MY BEDROOM WINDOW

After the cookies—I got to eat three, which is a lot of cookies to eat at once if they are big ones—it was time to go home. Mrs. Luther locked Crinkles in the kitchen with some food, then came with Sammy and me to the door.

Sammy was holding his jar of lion poop and was so happy, he couldn't stop smiling. Mrs. Luther had a new kind of cast that she could walk on, and it was not bright orange.

"Green, my favorite color," she said, pointing at her cast. "Like spring. How about you?"

"Brown," said Sammy. I was thinking it was probably because of poop, but Sammy said, "Like chocolate."

Then it was my turn: "Green, like tree leaves." I couldn't believe that Mrs. Luther and I had the same favorite color and for almost the same exact reason.

"Thank you both so much. I'm glad that you and Sammy are friends!"

"We're not friends," said Sammy, and he smiled at me and I could see bits of chocolate cookie stuck in between his teeth.

I said, "He's right, we're not," and I smiled back at him. But Mrs. Luther had closed her door so she could not hear us anyway.

Then Sammy walked home and I walked home and I thought, *Maybe he's got magnetic teeth. Maybe that's why food gets stuck there.* And I don't know why, but that made it seem a lot less disgusting.

Still Just Grace

For Ivy,
My empathy girl

ME

My real name is Grace, and if that was your real name then you would think that if someone wanted your attention they would shout "Grace!" but that is not what happens for me. I am not a usual person, but you can't tell that by just looking at me, because most of my unusualness is pretty much on the inside. My outside wrapping looks like any other girl's, except I don't wear very much pink because that is definitely not one of my favorite colors.

THINGS THAT ARE UNUSUAL
(SOME GOOD, SOME BAD, SOME NOT SURE)

1 Having four girls named Grace in the same class, and not letting any of them use the name Grace. Instead, calling them Grace W., Gracie, Grace F. (secretly named the Big Meanie by me, because that is what she is), and Just Grace. The Just Grace name probably being the most dumb name in the whole world ever, which is especially bad and sad because that's the one that is mine.

FOUR GRACES IN A ROW

ME   GRACE F. BIG MEANIE   GRACIE   GRACE W.

2 Thinking that someone is 100 percent disgusting and not likable, and then having something happen that changes your mind a little bit so that the gross disgusting feeling is almost all gone, even when you have to stand right next to him and say, "Hi, Sammy."

3 Having a little superpower that almost no one knows about. Empathy power is the power to feel someone else's sadness, and then to try to make that sadness go away. It's not an easy power to have. I know, because I have it.

USING MY EMPATHY POWER LAST WEEK
WHEN MOM MESSED UP DAD'S
BIRTHDAY CAKE

MOM, DON'T WORRY. DAD WILL LIKE IT, EVEN IF IT'S DROOPY.

It still tasted good, though!

 Girls who draw comics, because mostly that's a boy thing, though it just doesn't make any sense why it would be that way.

ONE OF MY NEW COMIC DRAWINGS

Butterfly Lady can make you feel better just by wrapping you in her big beautiful wings.

5 Living next door to your most perfect friend in the whole world. And having that friend be someone as great as Mimi.

ME AND MIMI

6 Having a cool French flight attendant named Augustine Dupre living right in your very own basement. But living in a great apartment that your dad made, not in the scary-spider part next to the furnace.

SPIDER

AUGUSTINE DUPRE

Hopefully they will never meet!

MYSTERY BOY
(SOUNDS BETTER THAN IT IS)

Mimi and I were watching the new people move into the house that the workers built right next door to her, where before there were just a bunch a weeds, broken glass, and prickle bushes.

NEW HOUSE MIMI'S HOUSE MY HOUSE

Actually, we were spying on them from her upstairs window, so they couldn't see us and we wouldn't have to talk to them.

Especially the mystery new boy who was going to be in our class. Mimi's mom was all excited about having new neighbors. She told Mimi she had to be nice to the new boy and let him play with us because he was going to be nervous and lonely. This did not sound like the kind of boy we wanted to play with. In my head I made a list of what could happen if you played with nervous, lonely creatures. It was not good.

LION   EAT YOU

BIRD   PECK YOU

DOG   BITE YOU

We saw the mom, the dad, and eight or nine moving people, but there was no boy. The moving people were like big ants and hard to count because they were all wearing the same blue shirt and not keeping still. "Maybe they left him at their old house," said Mimi. "Because he is terrible and they wanted to get rid of him," I said. "Because he is very gassy and has horrible breath," added Mimi. "And he burps and picks his nose!" I finished. "I'm glad he's not coming!" I said. "Me too!" said Mimi, and this made me secretly happy, because I did not want the new boy neighbor to be someone Mimi was going to like more than she liked me, her old girl neighbor.

MAGIC BOY
(STILL SOUNDS BETTER THAN IT IS)

Poof! Like magic, the next time we looked out the window we saw the boy. He was smiling and walking around the front lawn on his hands. He did not look nervous. The lonely part was hard to tell because that's an inside feeling so it's invisible. But most lonely people don't laugh and wave at strangers, which is what happened next, right after Mimi's mom pointed at the window where we were watching. Mimi's mom waved, the boy waved, and then they waited, looking at us, so we had to wave too. That's how the rule of waving works: you have to wave back if someone waves at you.

"He looks okay, like maybe he's fun,"

said Mimi. "I guess so," I said, but I looked out the window again just to make sure. "Oh, no! It's Sammy Stringer!" I cried. Sammy was talking to the new boy and Mimi's mom, and then Sammy was waving at us too. We waved, but then we made a pretend throw-up noise because you can't help but do that if something gets up there on your disgusto-meter.

MY DISGUSTO-METER CHART

HIGH
EATING A BUG ON PURPOSE.
EATING A BUG BY ACCIDENT.
STEPPING IN DOG POOP WITH BARE FEET.
SMELLING A SKUNK.
STEPPING IN DOG POOP.
SAMMY STRINGER.
MAYONNAISE ON A SANDWICH.
LOW

"We have to go down and say hello, or I'll get in trouble," said Mimi. "I know you hate Sammy Stringer, but you have to do this."

Then Mimi held my hand to give me some of her extra braveness. I used to hate Sammy Stringer. But now I just don't like him very much. It's not a big difference, and one day it might matter, but it didn't so much right then in that exact minute because I didn't want to talk to him, and, especially, I did not want him to call me Just Grace in front of the new boy.

SAMMY STRINGER SURPRISE

The first words out of Sammy Stringer's mouth were "Hey, Grace. Hey, Mimi. This is Max."

I couldn't believe that he didn't call me Just Grace, that he was being normal like a regular boy, and that his shirt wasn't covered in disgusting bits of food. This was all a big surprise for me. Mimi said hi. I said hi. Max said hi, and then Sammy said, "We're going to look at some stuff at Mrs. Luther's house."

Mrs. Luther is my neighbor on the side that is not next to Mimi's house. She is a teacher at our school, but she only teaches the kids that are older than us. Sammy likes her because she has collections of weird stuff like scary masks, animal poops, and other not regular stuff. And he probably also likes her because she makes amazing cookies that have real pieces of chocolate bars in them. I know about the cookies because I have tasted maybe ten of them, and they are excellent!

"Huh," said Mimi, and we watched them walk away. Sometimes when something completely unexpected happens your brain can't think of anything to say, so while your mouth is waiting for your brain it makes a little "huh" sound. So I knew what was happening in Mimi's head.

"Oh, well," I said. "That wasn't so bad." Sammy had been nice, Max had a new friend, and Mimi was still all mine. But maybe Mimi was thinking, *Now that fun handstand-walking Max boy won't be my new friend, and that disgusting and totally annoying Sammy Stringer is going to be hanging around next door.* I couldn't tell.

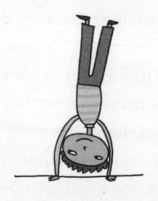

A PERFECT NIGHT

Mimi came over and we watched a new episode of *Unlikely Heroes,* which is our most favorite TV show ever. It's a show about real people who do things that usually only comic book heroes can do, and it's all 100 percent true.

This time there was a man who swam two whole miles in the ocean with a broken arm and a lady on his back. He had to save the lady when their boat tipped over because she couldn't swim and for some reason wasn't wearing a life jacket, which is a dumb thing to forget to wear if you don't know how to swim and you are on a boat in the middle of the ocean.

Then there was Sally, a pet parrot who pecked some robbers and kept them trapped in the house they were robbing until the police came to take them away. The owners of the parrot said Sally was a hero. Sally squawked, "Save me, Sweetie! Save me!" right on the TV, which is exactly what one of the robbers said when he was being attacked. The police said Sally was copying the robbers. Parrots love to copy sounds. Sally could also say, "Sally wants a biscuit" and "Hello, handsome," and make the beeping sound the microwave makes when the food is ready. Sweetie was the girl robber. They didn't say what the boy robber's name was. "Maybe Cupcake," joked Mimi.

WHAT IS GOING TO BE DIFFERENT AT SCHOOL

We are getting a student teacher for our class and his name is Mr. Frank. Mr. Frank is going to watch Miss Lois, our regular teacher, for a week, and then he is going to take over the whole class and teach it himself. Mr. Frank is a student teacher, which means he still goes to college, and still has to do homework, and is still mostly just learning about teaching stuff. This is good because it will be nice to have someone different and interesting for a change.

Miss Lois says student teachers have a lot of energy because they are young and fresh and full of new ideas. One of the new ideas I'm going to help Mr. Frank with is calling me Grace, or if I have to Grace S. for Grace Stewart. But I am definitely 100

percent not going
to help him call me
Just Grace!

HELLO, MR. FRANK, MY NAME IS GRACE.

WHAT WAS DIFFERENT AT SCHOOL

Mr. Frank was young and maybe fresh. I couldn't really tell that part, but the part I could tell right away was that Miss Lois was not going to let him use very many new ideas, especially when it came to changing names. As soon as I said, "Excuse me, Mr. Frank. I want to be called Grace or Grace S., please," Miss Lois said, "Now is not the time to be confusing everyone with new names." And then she said, "We will be keeping the same class name list even while Mr. Frank is here." Nobody seemed upset except me, but that is because I'm the only one with a stupid dumb name.

I looked over at Grace F. by mistake, and just like always, she was being mean. She was giving me a ha-ha smile right on her Big Meanie lips. Mr. Frank went around the room and introduced himself to everyone. I was not happy one bit when he said, "Hello, Just Grace. I'm happy to meet you," even though it's Miss Lois's rule and not his fault.

Once someone has started calling you one thing, it's almost impossible to get that person to change and call you anything different. So now of course I could tell that Mr. Frank was going to call me Just Grace forever and ever and ever. Even if I saw him on the street fifty-one years from now he was still going to say, "Excuse me, Just Grace, is that you?"

Then, to make everything even more worse, Mr. Frank kept calling Grace F. "Grace," instead of "Grace F." like he was supposed to. This was totally not fair to any of the other Graces, because Miss Lois said that no one could be called that. Grace F. seemed very happy that the mistake was happening and was all super chatty with Mr. Frank even though we didn't even know him yet. She was probably trying to put some kind of Big Meanie spell on him.

After lunch, Mr. Harris, the principal, brought Max to our class. He didn't get to sit next to Sammy because the only empty seat was the one next to the Big Meanie. I saw Sammy smile at Max, and then when none of the teachers was looking, Grace F. stuck her tongue out at Sammy. She probably thought he was smiling at her, which I know would never happen because even though Sammy

Stringer likes disgusting and unusual things, he would never in a billion years like anyone like the Big Meanie.

WHAT WAS DIFFERENT AT HOME

When I got home, I went right downstairs to visit Augustine Dupre. She is very good about making you feel better if something has happened that you do not like. She lets you talk and talk and talk until most of the unhappy feelings have been let out of your body in words.

JUST GRACE, SAMMY STRINGER, MAX, JUST GRACE, STILL JUST GRACE!

**COMPLAINY WORDS
COMING OUT OF
MY MOUTH**

Lots of people don't have time for this kind of thing, but Augustine Dupre is not a time rusher. When I finished telling her about how I was still probably going to be called Just Grace forever, she patted my arm and said, "Well, some time away will probably make you feel better." This is how I found out that I was going to miss three days of school and go on a trip to Chicago to visit my grandma.

WHY WE ARE GOING ON A VACATION AT A NOT NORMAL VACATION TIME

Mom says it is time for Grandma to move out of her house and into an apartment building, and that Grandma is going to be so much happier in a new, smaller apartment. She says there are lots of other old people living right in the same building, so Grandma won't be alone so much. She says they have movie nights, and dances, big dinners, and lots of art and music classes. It sounds a lot like summer camp except there are probably no bugs, and you don't have to go to a special building to use the bathroom.

I am thinking that maybe Grandma can make me a new wallet like the kind we made at camp last year, because my laces part got messed up and then the wallet couldn't open, which is not great because that is where the money is supposed to go. Plus, Grandma is good at sewing and making her fingers do exactly the right thing when they are holding string, or glue, or tiny little pieces of tape.

WALLET THAT GRANDMA COULD MAKE ME

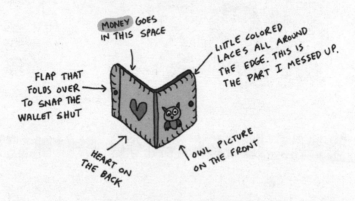

MONEY GOES IN THIS SPACE

LITTLE COLORED LACES ALL AROUND THE EDGE. THIS IS THE PART I MESSED UP.

FLAP THAT FOLDS OVER TO SNAP THE WALLET SHUT

HEART ON THE BACK

OWL PICTURE ON THE FRONT

WHAT IS SUPER EXCELLENT

Telling everyone at school that you get to miss school and go on vacation is one of the best things ever. It's more special than going when it's regular vacation time, because you are the only one who gets to do it and everyone else has to stay and work on boring school stuff.

WHAT IS NOT SUPER EXCELLENT

Miss Lois gave me homework to do while I was gone. So now I have to take the boring school stuff with me, which is not as fun as I thought it was going to be. The only okay part of the homework is the project to write a two-page story about something smaller than a peanut butter sandwich.

This was one of Mr. Frank's new ideas, and it seemed like a good one, except a lot of kids weren't listening and got confused. They thought we were supposed to write a story about a peanut butter sandwich. Marta, the girl with the longest hair in our whole class, said, "Excuse me, Mr. Frank, but I'm allergic to peanuts, so I shouldn't write about them because I might get sick and then have to get a shot."

Miss Lois didn't even let Mr. Frank answer. She said, "Now, children, forget about the peanut butter sandwich and just write a story about something that is smaller than this square." And then she drew a square that was the same size as a peanut butter sandwich on the chalkboard.

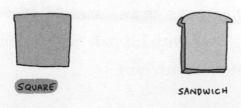

SQUARE

SANDWICH

Mr. Frank looked unhappy and his face got red. Grace F. was looking at Mr. Frank at exactly the same time as I was. It looked like she gave him a secret smile to try to make him feel better, but it must have been a mistake, because there is no way the Big Meanie could have even one drop of empathy power inside her.

MIMI AND MAX

After school I told Mimi all about my big surprise vacation. I said, "I'm sorry I won't be here to watch *Unlikely Heroes* with you tomorrow night," but she didn't seem very sad about my being gone.

"Oh, that's okay," said Mimi. "Max is coming over with his parents for dinner, so I can watch it with him."

This was not what I was wanting to hear, so I said, "What if he doesn't like it? Lots of boys don't like that sort of show because the heroes don't wear costumes or capes or even have big muscles." Mimi surprised me 100 percent by what she said next. "Don't worry," she said. "He loves *Unlikely Heroes,* just like us. I already asked him. Isn't that great?" "Yeah," I answered, "great."

But I wasn't being even 50 percent truthful, because great is getting lots of amazing super-surprise presents when it is not even your birthday. Great is not having your next-door-neighbor-best-friend-in-the-whole-world become best friends with her new next-door-handstanding-boy-neighbor while you have to go away on vacation.

SURPRISE PRESENTS

That night Mom said she had some surprise presents for me if I promised to be extra good on the drive to Chicago and not complainy when we drove by stuff that looked cool but didn't stop and get out of the car to see it. Stuff like a toothpick castle, a fairy land, a giant petrified forest, or even the world's largest sandwich. "Can I complain on the way back?" I asked. "No, it's a two-way deal," said Mom, and she held out a big sparkly bag with polka-dot tissue paper popping out the top. It's hard to say, "No deal," when you are looking at a bag filled with presents. So I said, "Okay, I promise."

The bag was filled with tons of great things, but the most excellent thing was the Supergirl underwear. It was exactly what I

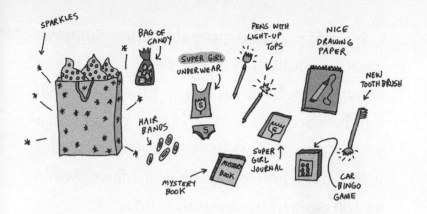

SPARKLES

BAG OF CANDY

SUPER GIRL UNDERWEAR

PENS WITH LIGHT-UP TOPS

NICE DRAWING PAPER

NEW TOOTH BRUSH

HAIR BANDS

MYSTERY BOOK

SUPER GIRL JOURNAL

CAR BINGO GAME

had always wanted, and the same kind that the girl on *Unlikely Heroes* wore when she rescued a grown-up man from drowning! I called Mimi up on the phone to tell her right away, and then I held them up at my bedroom window so she could look out her bedroom window and see them.

That's when I remembered that my window and Mimi's window would always be across from each other, and this could never happen with Max's window unless Mimi's whole house was turned completely around, back to front. Turning a house around is not easy and would probably not happen, because Mimi's dad is very careful and full of worry about his lawn all the time. He would not be excited about a house project that would ruin his grass. And if you turned a whole huge house around, your lawn would be 100 percent turned into mud.

TURNING MIMI'S HOUSE AROUND

THE DRIVE TO CHICAGO

We drove for a while and then Mom told Dad we had to stop for dinner or she was going to faint with hunger. I had pizza and then pie and ice cream, but mostly ice cream, for dessert. When we got back in the car it was dark, which made it really hard to see anything interesting. It is hard not to think about stuff in your head when there is nothing else to do, like look out the window. I had two big thoughts:

1 Was this vacation really going to be fun?

2 Was something important going to happen back at home while I was gone?

These are not the most perfect kinds of things to be thinking right before you fall asleep, but it is what happened. When I woke up it was morning and we were driving right into the big city of Chicago.

The Welcome to Chicago sign would be even cooler if it had your name on it.

Grandma lives right near the middle of the city. If I were older, Dad said it would only take me fifteen minutes to ride my bike from Grandma's house right to the entrance of the tallest building in the whole United States. Mom would never in a million years let me ride my bike on the road, so I would have to do it in secret. The tallest building is called the Sears Tower, and from the top you can see everything in Chicago, because Chicago's ground is as flat as a pancake.

FLAT AS A
PANCAKE

HILLY LIKE
MASHED POTATOES

MOUNTAINOUS LIKE
AN ICE CREAM SUNDAE

PROMISE

Right before we got to Grandma's house Mom asked Dad to park the car on the side of the road so she could talk to me without worrying about if we were going in the right direction or not. She said three things:

1 "This move is going to be hard for Grandma, so please try to be cheerful."

2 "If Grandma gives you something to keep, just take it and say thank you, even if you don't want it. We can throw it away later."

3 "Don't say anything about Grandma's new apartment building, Shady Grove, unless the something you are going to say is a nice thing."

Then Mom said, "Do you promise?" and I said, "Yes, I promise."

Dad started up the car and we drove two more blocks until we got to Grandma's house. Then we drove around and around and around, and finally we had to park in the same spot where Mom had made the promise talk because there weren't any other places to park.

It's really hard to find a parking spot in Grandma's neighborhood because lots of people like to go to there. There are amazing stores and restaurants all over the place.

MAP OF WHERE THE AMAZING THINGS ARE
THAT I KNOW ABOUT

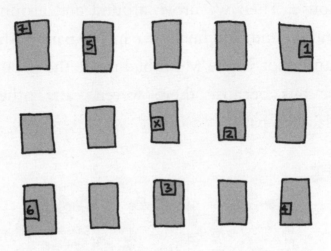

X Grandma's house.

1 Letizia's ice cream store/bakery (they have yummy everything!).

2 Store called Sparkly (everything in the whole store has sparkles on it). If you liked sparkles, then you would be crazy with joy the second you walked inside.

3 Lulu's Supply Shack — I am actually allowed to walk to this store by myself and buy stuff. They have normal things like cereal, milk, and candies.

4 Store that sells crazy lamps. It's fun to look in here even if you don't want to buy anything.

5 Comic book store — Grandma never lets me go in there because she said they only sell comics for grownups. It's on my list for when I'm grown up — I'm definitely going to go back there and go inside.

6 Coffee shop that has the best doughnuts in the whole world, even better than the doughnuts made in the doughnut store.

7 Art store. This is where I am sometimes allowed to buy art supplies when mine are all used up. If I were a famous artist I would for sure shop in here.

Two blocks is a long way to go if you have to carry lots of stuff, so it was good that we had the kind of suitcases with wheels. On the last block Mom raced me, but I won, so I got the first hug from the lady at the finish line. Of course it was Grandma.

MY FAVORITE THING ABOUT GRANDMA

Grandma always tells the truth, even if it could kind of hurt your feelings, which you might think is not good, but really it's okay, because she is not doing it to be mean. She just can't help it. She doesn't know how to tell a lie, even a teeny-tiny mini one. She says, "I've got truth serum in my veins—that's just how I was made."

It's kind of like my empathy power: sometimes it's a good power to have and sometimes it's not, but you can't pick and choose when you want it, because it's with you 100 percent of your whole life, which means always! And you have to live with it forever and let it be part of you, just like if you had big feet, stick-out ears, or long monkey arms. Except it is invisible, which is probably better, because people can't look at you and see it right away.

BIG FEET   **STICK-OUT EARS**   **LONG MONKEY ARMS**

THE SECOND THING GRANDMA SAID

The first thing Grandma said was "I'm so happy to see all of you." The second thing Grandma said was "I can't wait to move!" "Really?" asked Mom. "Really!" said Grandma, and I believed her because of the not lying power, but Mom, who has known Grandma her whole entire life, didn't seem sure. "Come on, I have a picnic in the backyard," said Grandma. "Race you," I yelled, but it really wasn't fair, because the first one through Grandma's side gate is always going to be the winner, and I was already there.

THINGS THAT ARE GOOD ABOUT PICNICS

Picnic food
Sitting outside
Cool air
Listening to the city

THINGS THAT ARE BAD ABOUT PICNICS

Ants

We had to move the picnic inside because Grandma's backyard is right on top of a giant underground ant farm. Grandma said they moved in last year and now the ant army is the biggest one she has ever seen. She said they probably can't wait until she leaves so that they can take over her house too! I especially don't like the big black ones. For some reason it's easier to squish a little ant than a big one. Grandma's ants were little, and she promised me that they did not go upstairs to where the bedrooms were. That was good news, because I did not want to worry about eating one when I was asleep. Not many people know this, but sleeping people eat bugs all the time. The bugs crawl into their mouth and then the sleeping people just swallow them up by accident. It's disgusting!

Mostly this happens with little bugs.

WHAT WE DIDN'T KNOW ABOUT GRANDMA

Mom was surprised, Dad was surprised, and I was surprised. Grandma has a new friend who is a man, and he is a great packer! Almost everything in Grandma's whole house was in a box with a colored label on it and very nice printing on the label. Grandma doesn't like to pack, which is why Mom and

Dad brought their work gloves and lots of markers and tape, but now they didn't need any of that stuff. Grandma told Mom and Dad that they should go out for dinner and not to worry about us because she had a pizza ready to pop in the oven. She was getting rid of them so we could have some special time together, which I was happy about. I love having Grandma all for me. Mom loved the idea too, but first she said I had to do my schoolwork while she asked Grandma some questions.

These were Grandma's answers:

"Two months ago."

"At the grocery store near the canned tomatoes."

"Roger Costello."

"Nice-looking, nice smile."

"Shady Grove."

"Nine grandchildren."

"It's just him and Captain Furry."

From where I was sitting I could only hear Grandma's part of the talking, but it wasn't very hard to figure out what most of the questions were. The Captain Furry one was a mystery, though.

← CAPTAIN HAT

CAPTAIN FURRY?

WHAT'S SO GREAT ABOUT TRENDY?

Mom said she and Dad were going to go somewhere fun and trendy. So I said, "What's so great about trendy?" Mom said that *trendy* was another word for popular, and that trendy restaurants were usually crowded with people who were famous, wished they were famous, or were hoping to see someone famous. She said there were at least ten trendy restaurants right near Grandma's house. After they left, Grandma said she didn't know anything about trendy but she knew what she liked, and what she was going to like after our pizza dinner was some tasty Italian ice cream. I said I was going to like that too!

WHAT WE TALKED ABOUT AT DINNER

I told Grandma all about still being called Just Grace, all about Mimi and Max, and all about Mr. Frank and the Big Meanie. It was a lot of stuff to tell, and it lasted from the first bite of pizza all through the walk to the bakery/ice cream store and right up until we were picking out our favorite flavors for dessert.

MY FAVORITES   **GRANDMA'S FAVORITES**

CHOCOLATE CHIP WITH BANANA

APPLE PIE

PISTACHIO

BANANA

PEACH

STRAWBERRY

LEMON

WHAT GRANDMA SAID

"The most important thing," said Grandma, "is to not be afraid of change. And sometimes change can be tricky. What looks like a bad change might really turn out to be a good change. It's always hard to tell at first—you have to let it sit for a while and see what happens." And then she said that being called Just Grace seemed a lot like a bad change and she was sorry about that. I was hoping she would tell me how to fix it, but she said she didn't know everything even though she had been around for a long time and was pretty old. I made a list in my head but I couldn't see how any of my bad changes were going to turn out to be good.

 Mr. Frank calling me Just Grace.

Mimi becoming best friends with Max.

The Big Meanie pretending to have empathy feelings and hating me at the same time.

SHE ALWAYS HAS HER HAIR DIFFERENT

WHAT WOULD HAVE BEEN GREAT

I know that this could never happen in real life, but I was hoping that Grandma would say, "I have just the thing to fix your problem," and then we'd go upstairs into her attic and she would give me a book with magic spells, a hypnotism ring, or some kind of special potion in a bottle, and then I would just follow some directions and everything could turn out exactly how I wanted.

WHAT GRANDMA GAVE ME

Some promises are harder to keep than other promises, but the promise to pretend to like what Grandma gave me was not even needed at all, because Grandma only gave me great stuff that I really for truly liked. Everything was in a box with my name scribbled in Grandma's messy handwriting on the side. I was glad that she made the box all by herself and didn't let her new packer man friend do it. My favorite thing in the whole box was Grandma's very own special silver heart locket on a chain. She said I could put a special picture in it and no one but me would know about it.

LOCKET GRANDMA GAVE ME

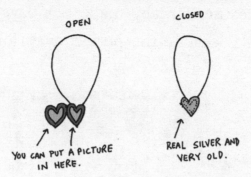

OPEN

You can put a picture in here.

CLOSED

Real silver and very old.

There was one special memory thing in the box. It was a poster I made for Grandma's dog Barnaby the time he ran after a squirrel and got lost by accident. We made sixty copies and put them everywhere we could think of until someone called and said he found him eating pizza out of a garbage can behind his house. Barnaby loved pizza crusts, which was good for me because that is the only part of the pizza I don't like. He died two years ago, and even though Grandma says she still misses him, she always smiles and laughs when we talk about him. She says it's because Barnaby made her days happy, which is exactly the perfect way for a pet to be.

The other stuff in the box was two wooden treasure boxes, a red velvet pillow with a map of Arizona sewn on the front of it, Mom's vest with all her Girl Scout badges, five big balls of colored string, a not real leopard skin purse — real leopard skin would be gross for me because I love animals — a scrapbook album from Grandma's trip to New York when she was fifteen, lots of pens with little things inside them that moved, and a Supergirl T-shirt. The T-shirt was new and not an old thing because Grandma said they didn't have Supergirls when she was young.

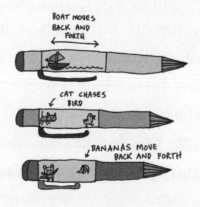

BOAT MOVES
BACK AND
FORTH

CAT CHASES
BIRD

BANANAS MOVE
BACK AND FORTH

TRENDY RESTAURANT

Mom and Dad were very excited about their dinner. They saw one famous person, the man who used to do the weather on the TV news. Plus they said the food was spicy and very good, which means I would not have liked it one bit. Mom said the walls of the restaurant were painted red and the windows had big velvety curtains on them. It sounded a lot like Augustine Dupre's living room, which would be a very nice place to eat dinner if you were not worried about spilling something on her white carpet. Dad said the restaurant did not have a white carpet on the floor, which was probably a good idea if you don't make people take their shoes off before they eat. Augustine Dupre has a no-shoe rule if you want to walk on her carpet; this is how she makes it stay nice and clean.

SUPER ME

Today I was Supergirl from my insides, which no one could see, to my outsides. I wore my new Supergirl underwear and my new Supergirl T-shirt both at the same time. The moving people got to the house really early and started putting everything with a red label on it into the truck. Grandma's packer friend was super good at organizing. He even made a color chart that explained all about the labels.

Green label means . . . donate it to someone needy, who might like it even if Grandma or no one in our family wants it anymore.

Red label means . . . Grandma is keeping it with her and taking it to her new Shady Grove apartment.

Yellow label means . . . it goes in the garbage.

Orange label means . . . Mom and Dad have to look at it and decide if they want to take it back home with us.

If they don't want it, they have to put on a new yellow label or a new green label.

While Mom and Dad looked at all the orange labels, I went upstairs to work on my story for school. For some reason all I could think about was ants, so it's a good thing that an ant is smaller than a peanut butter sandwich. Mr. Frank didn't say the whole story had to be just words, so I drew a comic, because one of my most favorite parts about making stories is the drawing pictures part.

STORY ABOUT SOMETHING SMALL

ANOTHER EASY PROMISE

Grandma's new Shady Grove apartment was fantastic, and I said that right after we finished getting the tour. Mom and Dad were smiling too, because the only things anyone could ever say about Shady Grove were great and amazing things. It was nothing like camp. It was fancy! And not fancy like you were scared to touch anything, but more just fancy like you wanted to say, "Wow! This is fancy." And then maybe do a twirl if nobody was watching. We all had breakfast with

Grandma and her new packer friend, Mr. Costello, in a covered garden outside. Mr. Costello was very nice but very furry. He had white fur all over his sweater and pants and even a bit sticking out of one eyebrow. I wanted to ask about it but wasn't sure if it was a nice question to ask or a not nice question to ask, so I didn't say anything. Eating outside was like a picnic except there were no ants, which is something Grandma was very happy about for sure.

NO WALLET FOR ME

After lunch we went to look at the arts and crafts room, where Grandma will get to make some projects. I asked the craft teacher lady if Grandma was going to make a beaded bookmark or a wallet but she said they didn't make that kind of thing. Instead Grandma can make paintings, or bowls, or even necklaces with real jewels. The craft lady gave me a cord necklace with an Indian bead head on it. It looked a little bit like something my next-door neighbor Mrs. Luther might wear, but I still liked it. I was only a little bit disappointed about the wallet, but I didn't say anything because mostly I was pretty happy.

WHAT WE DID THE REST OF THE DAY

We went to the zoo, which was great because it was free and that meant Mom and Dad had extra money for me to spend. I picked out two presents in the gift shop, one for me and one to bring back for Mimi.

VERY VERY
COZY. NOT
LIKE A REAL
POLAR BEAR

HANDS OPEN
AND CLOSE
SO MONKEY
CAN HOLD ON
TO STUFF

STUFFED POLAR BEAR FOR ME

MONKEY WITH PINCH PAWS FOR MIMI

After the zoo visit it was already lunchtime. Grandma wanted us to come back and have lunch with her and Mr. Costello, but Dad wanted to get a hot dog from his favorite Chicago hot dog restaurant. Mom said we should go back and eat at Shady Grove because this was a trip about Grandma and not a trip about eating hot dogs. This was easy for her to say because she doesn't like hot dogs very much anyway. Dad secret-whispered to me that we would get a hot dog before we left, PROMISE.

I asked Dad about Mr. Costello and why he was so furry but he said he hadn't noticed. I don't know how not, but sometimes grownups just don't see stuff. When I asked Dad if he knew anything about Captain Furry he said, "Is that one of the characters on that TV cartoon show that your mother doesn't like?" Obviously he didn't know anything at all. Maybe Captain Furry was a secret spy name for Mr. Costello? Maybe Captain Furry was a superhero who sprayed his enemies with fur, and Mr. Costello was an enemy? Maybe Captain Furry was something really amazing and cool?

INSIDES OUT

The new people who bought Grandma's house are going to take all the insides out of the house and throw them in the garbage, even the walls. Right after Grandma told me this she gave me a special photo book she made just for me. It was filled up with pictures of the inside of her house before everything was packed away. That way, Grandma said, I would never forget how it looked. Mom cried when she looked at the book, but it didn't seem sad to me. When Grandma saw Mom crying she started crying too, so I tried to do something cheerful to help them. I put Mimi's present on the end of my nose and pretended it wasn't there. I'm glad they looked and smiled right away, because the little monkey paws were pinching extra hard and making me have to breathe out of my mouth, which was not so easy, because it was filled up with turkey sandwich. After lunch Grandma took me to meet the mysterious Captain Furry.

CAPTAIN FURRY

Captain Furry is not a spy, not a superhero, and not something really amazing and cool. Captain Furry is a cat. A cat with crazy long hair who lives in the same apartment with Mr. Costello. I am glad I am not allergic to cats, because just looking at Captain Furry could make cat-allergic people sneeze and their eyes puff up like grapefruits — which are fruits I do not like, even with lots of sugar on them. Mr. Costello's living room is full of Captain Furry fur. Mr. Costello is full of Captain Furry fur. Even I was full of Captain Furry fur after only petting Captain Furry for just twenty seconds. You have to really be in love with a cat to live with that much fur in your world.

Captain Furry's best trick is that he jumps from the floor right up into Mr.

Costello's arms. Mr. Costello said that Captain Furry has lots of other tricks, like hiding in grocery bags and sleeping on pillows, but really those are just normal cat things and not tricks at all. But I didn't say that because I was trying to be polite.

NOT A TRICK

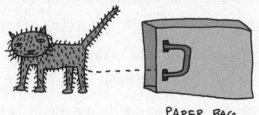

PAPER BAG

On our last night in Chicago we all went to a carnival: me, Grandma, Mom, Dad, Mr. Costello, and lots of Captain Furry's fur. The real Captain Furry had to stay home because cats can't go to carnivals. We found out about the carnival because there was a big poster for it right on the bulletin board near

Grandma's new arts and crafts room. Posters are a great way to get people's attention about stuff, because they are hard to miss seeing.

Mr. Costello says he brushes Captain Furry every week but still each time he gets enough fur on the brush to make a whole new mini Captain Furry.

CAPTAIN FURRY   BRUSH   MINI CAPTAIN FURRY

Dad and I went on most of the rides. Mom says she just likes to watch, which makes no sense, because I watched some of the big kids on the big rides and that was like having no fun at all. When I get taller there are two rides I am definitely going to go on for sure. One is called the Zipper and the other is called the Gravo-Force. On the Zipper you get to sit in a cage and spin all over like crazy; upside down, sideways, backwards, everything. On the Gravo-Force you stand up against the wall and get spun around really fast like you are in a washing machine and then suddenly the floor drops away from your feet. But the amazing thing is you don't fall down. You just stay there stuck up on the wall. And then when the ride slows down you just slide down the wall until your feet touch the floor again.

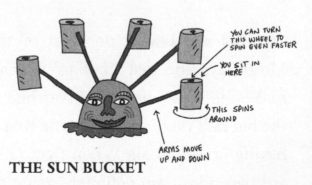

THE SUN BUCKET

My favorite ride that I went on.

I had so much fun I could hardly stand it! It would have been better if Mimi were there, but Dad was good about being my partner, and he didn't start feeling sick until the very last ride, which was the octopus and not even scary. Mom said we could have any kind of junk food we wanted for dinner. I had a hot dog, but Dad said it wasn't going to be the same as a hot dog from his favorite place. Dad didn't eat anything because he was feeling green, which means he was feeling like he might throw up.

Grandma and Mr. Costello didn't go on any rides, not even the Ferris wheel, which you can go on even if you are a tiny baby. Mr. Costello likes to organize and write labels, but he does not like high places. Grandma said she didn't mind staying on the ground with him even after Mom and I said she could ride with us. Grandma was being a good friend, because I know for sure that she likes being on the very top of the Ferris wheel a whole lot more than being on the boring ground.

It was one of the best vacation days ever in my whole life. At night we all slept in Grandma's new apartment, except for Mr. Costello and Captain Furry. They slept in their own apartment two floors higher up than us. Grandma said that Mr. Costello was not afraid of his apartment even though it was even higher up than hers. Grandma said it was because it was not tippy and swingy like the Ferris wheel and so that made it okay for him.

NOT A NORMAL BREAKFAST

For the whole trip I kept all the promises I made to Mom, which was not at all hard to do, and then right before we started driving home Dad kept his promise to me. We went to his favorite hot dog restaurant and had hot dogs for breakfast. We were the only ones there, because eight o'clock in the morning is not a usual time to eat a hot dog. It was strange but they still tasted pretty good. I only put ketchup on mine.

WHAT YOU ARE SUPPOSED TO PUT ON A CHICAGO HOT DOG

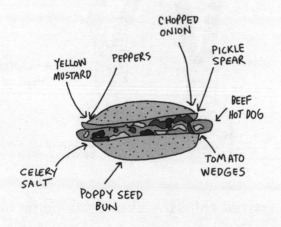

CHOPPED ONION

PEPPERS

YELLOW MUSTARD

PICKLE SPEAR

BEEF HOT DOG

CELERY SALT

POPPY SEED BUN

TOMATO WEDGES

THE DRIVE BACK HOME

I had hardly even thought about them when we were with Grandma, but as soon as we started driving back home all my problem worries rushed back into my head. I started thinking about Mimi and that handstanding Max. Maybe he was teaching her how to do it and now they were going to be handstanding new best friends.

MIMI WEARING HER FAVORITE PANTS

I started thinking about still being called Just Grace, and I started thinking about Mr.

Frank and the Big Meanie and her pretend empathy feelings. All the thinking made me wish that Dad would drive faster so we could get home sooner and I could find out if everything was just the same as when we'd left. I

MY BAD DRAWING

tried to draw, because that usually makes me feel better, but the car was too bumpy and I kept drawing squiggly lines by mistake. So instead I just had to play with Mimi's present.

Then I must have been asleep because Mom woke me up and said it was time to have some lunch. Grandma made us some sandwiches, but she forgot and put mayonnaise on mine, so I could only eat around the edges of it because mayonnaise is a food that is disgusting.

After lunch Mom and I played license plate bingo. I won all three games because she kept forgetting about playing and wasn't paying attention to the cars. Doing nothing sitting in a car makes you hungry a lot, so we stopped for dinner when it was only four-thirty, which is normally a time for snacks and not normally a time for a whole dinner. Dad said driving across the country is pretty boring. I think being the passenger when you are driving across the country is even more boring.

WHAT I SAW WHEN
I GOT HOME

Nothing. It was dark out and three in the-
morning and Mimi's house looked exactly
the same as always. It was not turned around,
which I was happy about.

WHAT I WANTED TO SEE ON MY
VERY OWN FRONT DOOR

WHAT I SAW IN THE MORNING

Sammy Stringer, Max, and Mimi all talking together on Mimi's front steps. Mimi looked surprised to see me, like maybe she forgot I was coming home, or maybe she didn't see our car parked in front of our house, which is pretty hard to miss because it is red and not silver or tan or black like most cars.

But then Mimi screamed my name and came running over, and it seemed like everything was going to be okay and normal. But I was 100 percent wrong! Max and Sammy followed Mimi's footsteps all the way across the yard until they were standing right next to us, which was not what I was expecting.

When Mimi and I went inside to get

SAMMY MAX MIMI

MIMI CHOO-CHOO

Mimi's present, Max and Sammy followed us through the front door, up the stairs, and right into my very own private all-girl bedroom. And the most surprising thing ever was that Mimi didn't even seem to notice. The only good part about it was that Mimi liked her present. Usually Mimi and I just stay in my room forever, but I did not want Sammy Stringer to sit on my bed or to even look at any of my special-to-me things, so I took Mimi back downstairs and into the kitchen before he could touch anything.

When Max saw the fridge, he said he was thirsty and asked for a drink. Of course I know how to be a good hostess so I gave everyone a big cup of orange juice with ice. Mimi asked me lots of questions about my vacation, but it wasn't as fun to talk about it when Sammy and Max were right there listening. Sammy saw my new bead-head necklace and said, "Hey, what's that? Is it from Mrs. Luther?"

I know it's not good to lie, but I couldn't help it, and plus this was a special bad occasion so I said, "No! It's a magic necklace. My grandma gave it to me." And then I said, "If I hold the bead head in my hands, close my eyes, and make a wish, then my wish will come true. Watch."

And then I closed my eyes and made a pretend wish that he would leave.

"What'd ya wish for?" asked Max. "Yeah, I don't see anything different," said Sammy. "It's like birthday wishes," I said. "You have to keep the wish a secret!" It was unbelievable how they could not see even one little bit how annoying they were being to me. "Well, I believe you," said Mimi, and then she said, "Do you want to come over after lunch and watch *Unlikely Heroes*?" "Sure," I said, and that made me feel happy again. But then both Max and Sammy said "Sure" too, and I was not feeling so happy again after all. "Great!" said Mimi. "See you later." And then they walked out the door all together. And Sammy was gone just like I wished he would be, except that Max and Mimi were gone too. The Mimi-being-gone part was not what I wanted at all.

WISH NECKLACE

When something happens that is strange or unusual but not magic it is called a coincidence. A coincidence is having no money and really wanting ice cream, and then finding fifty cents on the sidewalk, which is the perfect amount to buy a soft cone from the ice cream truck, which just happens to drive by in the next minute. Actually, that would really be two coincidences put together, which would be even more unusual and amazing.

1 Finding the fifty cents on the sidewalk.

2 The truck driving by right then.

These kinds of things do not happen very often, so when they do, most people who are good at paying attention, notice them. Wishing on the bead head and having the wish maybe come true was probably a coincidence, but I made another wish to test it out, just in case it really was filled with magical power. I closed my eyes and, holding the bead head the exact same as before, I wished for a swimming pool right in my very own backyard. This would be an excellent wish to come true, since swimming is one of my five most favorite things to do for exercise. I hardly ever get to swim because the only swimming pool I can go to is three miles away from my house and that is way too far for me to ride on my bike. That's what Mom says, and she gets to be the boss of me about stuff like that until I'm all grown up.

When I opened my eyes the yard was still filled with only grass and weeds, just like always. No swimming for me. But I kept the bead-head necklace on, because even pretend magic could maybe be better than no magic at all.

HELP WANTED

What I really, really needed was to be wearing my Supergirl underwear so I could have an amazing idea about how to make Sammy and Max disappear from Mimi, but Mom hadn't finished the laundry yet from our vacation, so I couldn't. And even though I thought about it real hard, all the time through lunch, my brain couldn't think up anything good. I tried to draw a comic to make myself feel better, but that didn't work either.

After lunch I walked over to Mimi's house because being with Mimi, Max, and Sammy was still better than being all alone without Mimi. Plus I didn't want to miss *Unlikely Heroes*. Maybe if Max and Sammy didn't talk while we were watching I could pretend they weren't even there.

WHAT MIMI SAID

Max and Sammy left after we watched three whole episodes of *Unlikely Heroes*. Mimi and I had seen them all before, but that's okay because they were still good. They were new for Max and Sammy, which made them not true *Unlikely Heroes* fans, because if you watched the show every week you would for sure have seen those episodes already.

I was secretly wondering about Max being an *Unlikely Heroes* fan when Mimi said, "Can you believe Max only ever saw *Unlikely Heroes* one time before he moved here?" It was probably another one of those coincidences, but I was holding the bead head right when she answered my thought question.

I wanted to ask Mimi why Max and Sammy were following her around so much, but this was not an easy question to ask. I touched the bead head, hoping that it would make her give me the right answer again. She said, "That Sammy Stringer really isn't so bad once you get to know him. I don't even think he picks his nose anymore, because I would notice something like that and I haven't seen him do it." This was not the right answer.

Then she said, "Max is teaching us and we can almost do walking handstands like him." This was not the right answer either, and especially not something I wanted to hear, because I can't even do a standing-still handstand, or a cartwheel, or anything where the arms of the body are supposed to hold up the whole rest of the body.

Mimi asked me to stay for dinner, but then I couldn't and had to go home because her eyes puffed up and she started sneezing over and over again. It looked like she was allergic to me, but her mom pointed at my shirt and said it was probably just the cat fur.

WISH

When I went home I had one big wish, but the necklace was for sure not going to be able to help.

I wished I hadn't gone away on vacation, but then at the last minute I changed it because then I wouldn't have seen Grandma in her new apartment. And when I'm talking to her on the phone or thinking about her I like to be able to know exactly where she is. It makes her seem not so far away.

After dinner I tried to do a handstand, but that didn't work out like it was supposed to either.

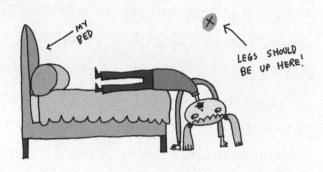

MR. FRANK'S NEW IDEA

While I was away on vacation I missed a lot of Mr. Frank's new ideas. He had even more new ideas today, but none of them had anything to do with not calling me Just Grace, because as soon as I walked into the classroom he said, "Welcome back, Just Grace."

The new idea that I didn't miss, and I wish I did miss, was that the whole class had to pair up with partners and come up with a project that had something to do with language. This sounded like it could maybe be a project about talking, but if you thought that you would be wrong. Mr. Frank's language project had to be about words, letters, or communication (which is a word that means how information goes from one person to another person). You weren't allowed to just stand in front of the class and talk about stuff or sing the alphabet song — those kind of things didn't count. Mr. Frank said we had to use words that were written down. Plus he said he wanted to see some creativity. Not everyone was happy, especially Abigail Whitkin, because right away she started to whine about not being able to sing the alphabet song for her project. She is one of those people who knows how to sing the whole thing backwards, which is not amazing but still kind of cool. So it would have been easy for her to show off her talent in front of the whole class and not do any extra work.

But the most terrible part of all was that while I was gone on my vacation, everyone had already picked their project partners. Mr. Frank asked everyone to stand in their groups, and that's when I saw Mimi and Max and Sammy all standing together. Mr. Frank said I had to join a group that had only two people in it. There was only one two-person group in the whole class, and it was the one group I would have never picked even in a million years. Having your teacher stand right next to you can make your feet do things they wouldn't normally want to do, so my feet walked across the room and stood next to Grace W. and the Big Meanie. It made my insides feel unhappy from head to toe!

Big Meanie Bossy-Pants

The Big Meanie was horrible and wanted to do all of the deciding about what the project was going to be all by herself. Mr. Frank said we had to pool our talents and our interests, which means we had to find a project that we all liked and could do all together, but the Big Meanie was not listening. Her big idea was that we should make a hair salon and give everyone in the class fancy hairstyles. This was a dumb idea and one that was not pooling our talents because Grace W. and I don't know anything about fancy hair and always wear our hair in exactly the same way every single day. Plus boys don't like anyone to mess with their hair and make them look all pretty. The Big Meanie said we could make up one hairstyle for each letter in the alphabet. Then she gave us both a piece of paper with drawings of girls' heads with different hairstyles on it. She said, "Just Grace, Grace W., pay attention!"

I didn't want to say it but the first thing

I thought about when I saw the paper was *Wow! The Big Meanie is even better at drawing than I am.*

Then she said, "You two have to practice some of these hairstyles tonight. And I'll think of the creative alphabet names." She was being 100 percent bossy, so I said, "You are not the boss of me!" Both Mr. Frank and Miss Lois looked over because I think I said it kind of loud, and we would have for sure gotten in trouble if the Big Meanie hadn't made a pretend smile and put her arm over my shoulder like we were best friends, which for sure we were not! "Quick, look happy," said the Big Meanie, and both Grace W. and I made pretend smiles. She was being bossy again but this time it seemed like maybe it was for a reason, so we let her. Just to see what was going to happen next.

REAL SMILE   **PRETEND SMILE**

If you know someone really well you can tell the difference.

MR. FRANK

The Big Meanie told us all about Mr. Frank and how she didn't want him to get into any more trouble with his new ideas not working out. She said that Mr. Frank had tried lots of new ideas but that Miss Lois wasn't looking like she liked most of them, and when Miss Lois didn't like an idea she took the class back from Mr. Frank and that made his face get all red and sad.

In two weeks Miss Lois was going to give Mr. Frank a grade just like she gave us, and if she gave him something bad like an F or a D then he would never get to be a teacher and would probably have to go work at the grocery store at night, putting boxes and cans on the shelves.

GOOD GRADES   **OKAY GRADES**   **BAD GRADES**

The Big Meanie said this was why we had to pretend to be liking each other and liking the project. I was very surprised, but she was right: this was a very good reason. I looked at Mr. Frank and I could tell he looked unhappy, or maybe he was just mad at Abigail Whitkin because she had started humming the alphabet song. If someone is humming the alphabet song, your brain just wants to sing along and you can't make it stop, no matter how hard you try. It's annoying! Right then I felt sorry for him and my empathy power just started right up. "We have to help him," I said, and then I let both of the Graces tell me about some of Mr. Frank's not-working-out new ideas that I had missed when I was away on my vacation.

MR. FRANK'S NEW IDEAS THAT MISS LOIS DIDN'T LIKE

1 Saying that anything with words on it can be used in reading class. Miss Lois says magazines and comic books do not count for reading, and she was very not happy when John Traffie brought in three cereal boxes with puzzles on the back for his reading project.

2 Having everyone in the class make up a new crazy name for themselves with this formula that was supposed to help us learn about the different parts of a sentence:

An adjective (which is a describing word) + a participle (which is an action word and kind of a verb) + the first letter of your name added to "umble" if it's a consonant or the first letter of your name added to "cky" if it's a vowel + a noun (which is a thing) + the name of some kind of pastry.

ADJECTIVE + PARTICIPLE + − UMBLE OR −CKY + NOUN + PASTRY NAME

Miss Lois especially didn't like Brian Aber's made-up name, which was

Slimy Oozing Bumble Butt Cake.

My name would have been something much more creative and beautiful, but after a couple of the boys used endings like Booger Pie and Poop Cookie Miss Lois said the name project was over, so I didn't get a chance to make up a name. Poop Cookie sounded a lot like something Sammy Stringer's brain would think up.

**WHAT GIRLS
THINK UP**

**WHAT BOYS
THINK UP**

3 Asking the class to draw something from their imagination that they wished was real. Kids drew superheroes, and fairies, and friendly monsters and stuff like that, but when Isabella drew a unicorn Sandra Orr said, "You can't draw a unicorn! Unicorns are real! You have to pick a made-up thing!" Mr. Frank came over and told Sandra that he was pretty sure that unicorns were not real, but then Sandra started to cry and said that her mom had seen one so he was wrong, they were real!

Sandra was crying so hard, Miss Lois had to take her out of the classroom and walk her to the nurse's office. When Miss Lois came back she said everyone should put the imagination creatures away and just draw a favorite zoo animal instead. Grace W. said Mr. Frank's face was very red.

Nobody said anything more about unicorns for the whole rest of the day, and when Sandra came to school today she was  wearing a white sweatshirt with a unicorn and a rainbow on it.

THREE GRACES

I was pretty sure that it wouldn't work, but I held on to the bead head just like before and wished that Mr. Frank would be okay. I wished that his face would not get red because of this new idea, and I wished that he would not have to get a job putting cans and boxes on the grocery store shelves at night. I made all my wishes for Mr. Frank because he seemed to need wishes more than I did, and now I was filled with empathy power for him.

The Big Meanie saw me closing my eyes and said, "Grace, what are you doing?" I was 100 percent surprised that she called me Grace and not Just Grace like she normally did. It was like she forgot that she was the Big Meanie and filled with hate for me.

I said, "I'm just trying to think of how to help Mr. Frank and come up with an idea for our project that uses all of our pooling of talents. Grace and I don't know anything about hairstyles." I thought she might be mad, but she just looked at both of us and then said, "Grace, I see what you mean." And for some reason, that just made us start calling each other Grace as much as we could. It was confusing but very fun. "So, Grace, what do you think we should do?" "I don't know, Grace. How about something big?" "Grace, do you think Grace means a big sign or some kind of huge poster?" "Yes, Grace, I think Grace does. Let's do something that will get everyone's attention, okay, Grace?"

All this Grace talking made me sad that we couldn't use our normal Grace names like this all the time, and I said, "I sure wish I wasn't called Just Grace. It's unfair that I lost my real name!" "Mine too!" said Grace. "And mine three," said Grace. And then right there, because of everything we had just said, I had the start of an idea.

THE PROJECT IDEA

Grace and Grace loved the idea. And we made a promise to keep it a three Grace secret until we were ready to show everybody what it was.

SURPRISE

Mimi said she was sorry that I couldn't be in her group with Max and Sammy. Then she said she was sorry that I had to be in a group with the Big Meanie and I said, "Grace F. isn't really a big meanie all the time." "I'm surprised," said Mimi, and I could tell that she really was.

MIMI'S PROJECT

Mimi said that she and Max and Sammy were doing a human alphabet for their project. She said that she was trying to keep it a secret to surprise me, but that now that she could almost do a handstand she couldn't make herself not tell me. She said that handstanding was important because they were going to make their bodies be all the letters of the alphabet, from A to Z and then shout out all the adjectives they could think of that started with that letter. Mimi said that some of the letters were harder than others and right now they had practiced all the way to *K*, which was kind of a hard one. She said the letters were pretty easy to do if you did them lying down on the ground but a lot harder when you did them standing up, which is what they were going to do. She said it was lucky that Max was so good at handstanding because that helped a lot.

HOW THREE BODIES COULD MAKE A *K*

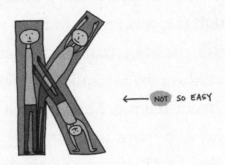

← NOT SO EASY

Right when Mimi was about to ask me what my project was going to be she started sneezing. She pointed to my shirt and I could see that it had Captain Furry fur on it. How or why is a mystery, because it was a clean shirt that hadn't even gone on the trip with me to Chicago. In between sneezes Mimi said that I could come to her house after school and watch her, Max, and Sammy practice the *L* and *M* and *N* part of the alphabet. "I'll try," I said, and suddenly it didn't even make me super sad that Mimi was going to be with Max and Sammy again. Because now I knew the real reason they were being together all the time. You can't be a human alphabet without practice. Mimi was just busy with her project, just like I was going to be busy with the other Graces.

WHAT WAS LUCKY

It was lucky that Mimi started sneezing at the exact time she did, because I didn't want to have to say, "I can't tell you what my project is because it is a three Grace secret." Plus I didn't want to tell her why I was going to have to go to the grocery store after school and ask for nineteen empty boxes.

Nineteen boxes = one for everyone in the class, even Mr. Frank and Miss Lois.

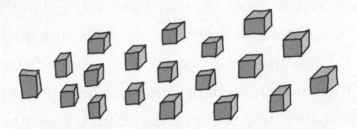

IF YOU LEARN A LESSON YOU SHOULD TRY NOT TO FORGET IT

If you get in trouble with your parents for something, it is a good idea to try to remember what it was for so you don't make that exact same mistake again another time. Once I got into trouble for walking all over my neighborhood without permission, so now I know exactly what to do. This time I asked Mom first. Mom said she would walk with me to the grocery store, but then Augustine Dupre was standing outside and said she needed to go too. I guess Mom didn't really want to go, because when she heard this, she gave me some money and a list of two things to buy and a quick goodbye wave.

Augustine Dupre said, "You must be buying a lot of groceries if you need to bring that wagon. How many things are on your list?" "Two," I said. "Just strawberry jelly and mustard. The wagon is for the empty boxes. I need nineteen of them." And then I told Augustine Dupre all about the project. It was

breaking the Grace secret, but Augustine
Dupre was not going to tell anybody one
word about it because she is the number one
best secret keeper I have ever met. She said,
"What an interesting idea." And that made
me happy because I thought so too.

When we got home it was almost dinnertime and too late to go over to Mimi's
house. I didn't see her or even hear anyone in
her yard, so they were probably already all
finished with the alphabet practice.

FANCY HANDWRITING

After dinner I took all the boxes into
Augustine Dupre's apartment. Augustine
Dupre can do perfect fancy handwriting
just like Grandma's new friend Mr. Costello,
so I asked her to write the numbers

on the front of the boxes for me.

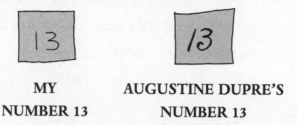

| MY | AUGUSTINE DUPRE'S |
| NUMBER 13 | NUMBER 13 |

When we were finished Augustine Dupre helped me put all the boxes in Mom's car so Mom could drive me to school with them tomorrow. Augustine Dupre is always helpful and thoughtful and filled with energy, just like Mr. Frank and even Grandma. Even though Grandma is kind of old and doesn't have much running-around energy, she is filled with lots of helpful energy. Plus, she is smart, because right now some of my bad changes looked like they were maybe turning into good changes, just like she said they could. And the most surprising one was about the Big Meanie, who had stopped being a Big Meanie right in front of my very own eyes. When I told her, Grandma wasn't going to hardly believe it!

WHAT I FORGOT

The next day I was so excited about bringing my boxes to school that I forgot to check my clothes to make sure they did not have any Captain Furry fur on them. I remembered about that part after I was talking to Mimi and she started sneezing. She wanted to tell me all about being a human *W* but I had to move away from her and then Miss Lois got mad and said, "No shouting in the hallway." If there are yes-people and no-people, Miss Lois is for sure in the no-person group. Mr. Frank is a yes-person.

Grace who used to be the Big Meanie said that Mr. Frank is her most favorite teacher ever and that she knows a secret about him but she is not allowed to tell it to anyone at school. I asked if she could tell us the secret if she was not at school and maybe at my house instead. When she said, "I think so," I invited both the Graces to my house after school.

WHAT IS IMPOSSIBLE

It is impossible to pick every piece of Captain Furry fur off your shirt. As soon as you let

it go with your fingers it flies right back and lands somewhere else on your shirt.

Because of this happening I couldn't sit next to Mimi at lunch. It is impossible for a person to chew and swallow a sandwich while she is sneezing so I sat in the middle of Grace and Grace instead. I forgot that I was wearing my bead-head necklace until I saw Mimi sitting all alone at her table. As soon as I saw her sadness I closed my eyes and wished for Max and Sammy to sit with her, which was a wish I would have never thought that I would make. Not ever. Then like magic I saw Sammy and Max walk over to Mimi with their lunch bags. Mimi saw me looking at her and waved with a big smile on her face like maybe she knew about my wish. But she couldn't have, because Mimi is not a mind reader and I know that for sure. And even though my wishes were happening all around me like crazy, it was probably just another one of those coincidences.

Right then the Grace who used to be the Big Meanie asked if she could wear my bead-head necklace for a while. I was going to say, "No, my grandma gave it to me," but then I remembered about that part not being true. Grandma hadn't given me the bead-head necklace; she'd given me her special silver locket, which I had 100 percent forgotten all about. The bead head was from the craft lady, so it really wasn't special except for maybe being magic, which it probably wasn't anyway. It took a long time to think about all this stuff, which for sure made Grace think I was trying to think up a nice way to say no. She seemed really surprised when I said yes and took it off to give it to her.

THE PROJECT AT SCHOOL

In the afternoon Mr. Frank reminded everyone that the next day was going to be the start of the project presentations. We all already knew this because he had said the same thing right before we all went to the lunchroom for lunch. He seemed nervous that the class was going to mess up another one of his new ideas, but he didn't have to worry about us.

We three Graces were ready for our project. I had the boxes with the numbers already done and sitting in the cloakroom, and the other Graces had finished their parts of the project too. Grace had written each number (1 to 19) on a little card and Grace had made the special posters at the copy store. We decided that Grace should make the posters because she was so good at drawing, and even though we didn't use her idea for the hair salon, we still thought that the hairstyles drawings she made were pretty excellent.

At the end of class Mr. Frank came over and asked us how we were doing with our project. By mistake he called Grace "Grace" again and not Grace F. like he was supposed to, but this time it didn't make me grumpy like before.

SOMETHING NEW AT MY HOUSE

I had never before in my life had anyone else with the name of Grace in my house, and then today there were three of us. I introduced each new Grace to Mom and she said, "Oh my, this is a little bit confusing. How does this work at school?" But before either of the other Graces could answer I said we had to go upstairs to work on some homework.

I didn't want Mom to know that my name at school was Just Grace. It was exactly the kind of thing that would make her mad, and then she would go to the school and complain. And even though I 100 percent don't like the name Just Grace, having Mom come to the school all angry about it would be worse. Only babies complained about stuff like that to their mom, and I was not a complainer baby!

MY ROOM

I let the other Graces sit on my bed and even touch my things, and it did not bother me

one little bit. Grace had the bead-head necklace on and I told her she could still keep it
for a while if she wanted, then I asked her
about the Mr. Frank secret.

**GRACE HOLDING
MY NEW ARIZONA
PILLOW**

THIS IS NICE!

THE BIG SECRET

Grace asked me to close my bedroom door
so no one else could hear and then she said
the big secret was that Mr. Frank was an
alien. Both of us other Graces screamed, "AN
ALIEN?" at the exact same time.

Then the Grace who used to be the Big Meanie started laughing and said no, she was only joking, but that Mr. Frank being an alien would be way more exciting than the real true secret. She said the real true secret was that Mr. Frank was her very own next-door neighbor, and that before he was Mr. Frank the student teacher he used to be called Jeffrey. And that last summer when he was still Jeffrey, he had even baby-sat her and her little sister, Annie, two times. She said that she was really good at calling him Mr. Frank but that he was always forgetting to remember to call her Grace F.

We other two Graces smiled when she said that because it made us feel a whole lot better to know the reason Mr. Frank was always making that mistake. It's harder for old people to change to new ideas. Young people like us can do it much better. Grace told us all about the things she knew about Mr. Frank, and of course we promised not to ever say even one word about any of it to anyone.

THINGS ABOUT MR. FRANK

1 He used to have a girlfriend named Rebecca, but now Grace never sees her anymore.

2 He is really good at playing basketball and almost always makes the basket.

3 He likes to wear T-shirts with the names of rock groups on them when he is not working at our school.

4 He has a dog named Winkie. It is a golden retriever, but Winkie is pretty fat, so he doesn't look so much like a regular golden retriever.

5 He loves to wear his base-ball cap, which has a picture of a tractor on the front of it.

Grace said Mr. Frank is a nice neighbor, and then both of us other Graces said we thought Mr. Frank was a nice teacher too. I was sure hoping that our project would work out great and he could stay a teacher forever.

All this talking about Mr. Frank being Grace's neighbor made me think about my very own neighbor Mimi, and how I never got to even stand next to her anymore because there was fur stuck on everything

I owned. As soon as the Graces left, I got out the vacuum so I could suck up every single piece of Captain Furry fur in my whole entire room. I had to set the vacuum to the super-suck level, because once a piece of Captain Furry fur is on something it sticks there like it is glued. After cleaning I sat down and drew a new comic because it seemed like forever since I had done one and it is something I really like to do.

MORNING

I asked Mom to make French toast for break-fast because when my empathy power is working super hard this is what I like to eat. Plus, today was going to be the best day ever because I was wearing my Supergirl under-wear, Grandma's silver locket, and a shirt and pants with not one single piece of Captain Furry fur anywhere. I know this because I checked it in the mirror two times, two times, which is four, to be extra sure.

FUR-FREE ME

PROJECT DAY

As soon as we got into the classroom, Mr.

Frank said we had to go stand with our group partners. Then one person from each group had to pick a number from a baseball hat. We three Graces all smiled because the hat Mr. Frank was using had the picture of a tractor on the front of it, and that meant it was his favorite hat. I went to pick the number and got number three. This was excellent, because for our project to work right we had to start it in the morning and then not finish it until later in the afternoon.

THE PROJECTS

The first group to do their project was the group of Trevor, Ruth, and Francis. All the boys like Ruth because even though she is a girl, she pretty much likes to do boy things more than girl things. But their project was not just a boy thing. They had a huge pile of mixed-up magnetic letters set up next to a big magnetic tray, a dictionary, and a timer clock.

Francis said that they were going to spell out six words in six minutes and that the audience, which was us, got to pick out the words. Everyone started shouting out words at the same time until Mr. Frank said we all had to calm down and take turns. Once we had told them all the words, Trevor pushed the timer button and they started. Ruth had to look in the dictionary to make sure they'd spelled everything the right way.

It was pretty exciting, and near the end of the time we all started chanting, "Go, go, go," and Mr. Frank and Miss Lois didn't even tell us to stop. They got all the words on the board with only ten seconds left over. It was a great project! I could tell that even Miss Lois thought so because she was smiling.

THEY SPELLED SOME
REALLY GOOD WORDS

The next group to do their project was Mimi, Max, and Sammy. Mr. Frank looked a little surprised when they took off their shoes and socks, but he didn't say anything. Max told the audience, us, that he and Mimi and Sammy were going to make each letter of the alphabet using their bodies and then shout out as many adjectives as they could think of that started with that letter. I couldn't believe how good they were. You could really tell that they had practiced.

THE
AMAZING MIMI

My favorite letter was the N because that was the one where Mimi was upside down doing a handstand, and that was a new trick for her and not at all easy to do.

After the Z and "zany" everyone clapped like crazy and Mimi and Max and Sammy all smiled like crazy. And the whole time I even forgot that I used to think that Sammy was disgusting. While they were putting their socks and shoes back on, Grace, Grace, and I got ourselves organized. We even had a name for our project: it was called What You Lost, which was a pretty excellent name because everybody loses stuff, even rich and famous people.

WHAT YOU LOST

Grace went around the room and gave everyone, even the teachers, a little piece of paper with a number on it. Everyone was going to be part of our project. We told them all to keep their number secret and then the other Grace gave everyone one of the posters she had made. They looked really nice. She made three different kinds so not everyone got the same one.

 WE MADE CUTS SO THAT THE LITTLE BOTTOM TABS COULD BE TORN OFF

After that I put all the boxes in a line at the front of the room. Each box had its own beautiful number on the front and a little slit in the top where you could put a note.

EXAMPLE OF SOME OF THE NOTE BOXES

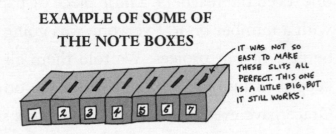

IT WAS NOT SO EASY TO MAKE THESE SLITS ALL PERFECT. THIS ONE IS A LITTLE BIG, BUT IT STILL WORKS.

I could tell that no one had any idea of what we were going to do, which was fine because we were going to explain everything and they were going to love it. I was kind of nervous when I went in front of the class. But when I looked at my two Graces, they made the G sign that Grace who used to be the Big Meanie had just invented that very morning, and seeing that gave me the extra braveness I needed.

HAND G SIGN

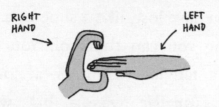

RIGHT HAND →

← LEFT HAND

So I took a big breath and said, "This is called the What I Lost project, and it is about communication . . . the written-down kind. We gave each and every single one of you your very own poster." And then I looked at Miss Lois and Mr. Frank, because we had given them one too. I learned that from Miss Lois. If you want to get someone's attention in a class, you have to give that person the teacher stare. And I wanted Mr. Frank and Miss Lois to notice that we were the only group ever who was including them right in our project with the rest of the class. Then I continued with the explaining part. "On every poster there is a blank space where you have to write down the name of something that you have lost, like a shoe or a button or anything you can think of. You can write about a tangible thing or a not tangible thing." *Tangible* was a big word that Augustine Dupre helped me with, and one that I was sure was going to impress Miss Lois. I told everyone what it meant because *tangible* is not a word that most kids can understand without some explaining to help them. "A *tangible* thing is something that you can hold or feel." And then I wrote some examples on the board so everyone could understand.

TANGIBLE	Not TANGIBLE
CHAIR	FEELINGS
HAIR	DREAMS
SHIRT	WISHES
CAR	RAINBOWS
APPLE	
HORSE	

I almost wrote down *unicorn* under the not tangible list. It was good I remembered about Sandy, because she would have for sure cried about that again.

Then I filled out my Lost poster right in front of them all so that they would know exactly what to do when it was their turn. "See, right under the word *lost* you write in something you have lost. Like I just did." Lots of kids in my class don't pay attention, so it's a good idea to explain stuff really carefully, as if you are talking to someone in kindergarten or something.

**WHAT I WROTE
ON MY POSTER**

When I was finished everyone said "Ooohh" and looked at Miss Lois. She was smiling only a little tiny smile, but still she didn't look mad, so this was a good thing. Then it was time to explain the very end part of the project. I held up my little secret number card so everyone could see it. It had a number 11 on it. I showed them all where to write their secret numbers on their posters. I wrote my number in the square at the top of my poster and on the six little squares on the bottom of the poster.

"Now what?" asked Ruth. Miss Lois made her teacher hand sign that means "If you have a question, please put up your hand." Ruth looked at Miss Lois and then put her hand up. Just like Miss Lois, I pointed at her and said, "Yes?" and she said, "What happens now?"

It was a good question because that was exactly the next thing I was going to talk about. So I said, "Well, when everyone has finished the posters we are going to hang them up all around the class so everyone can walk around the room and read them. When you see a poster that you want to write something about, you pull off one of the little pieces of paper at the bottom and write your message on it. Then you take your message over to the box with the same number on it and drop it inside."

"It's just like the boxes we use on Valentine's Day," shouted Sammy, "except those ones have your name on the front." Mr. Frank said, "Sammy," and Miss Lois gave him her teacher look because he had broken two school rules at the same time, shouting and not putting his hand up. But he was right about the valentines boxes. And it was a good way to explain it to the class. I smiled at him even though he had interrupted me and then gotten in trouble. Mimi could be right — maybe Sammy was kind of okay. Plus, I hadn't seen him pick his nose in ages, which was definitely a good thing.

Sandra Orr put her hand up so I said, "Yes?" and pointed at her. "Can we write more than one message? What if we see two posters we want to write about?" I was glad it was an easy question to answer, and I said, "You can write as many messages as you want."

Then I pointed at Robert Walters because his hand was up too. "Why do we have to keep our posters a secret? What if I want everyone to know it's about me and I wrote it because it's so excellent?" This was a harder question to answer, but I thought about it for a minute and then said, "It's just a rule so no one will get embarrassed." Robert was not my favorite person in the class. He always thought everything he did was wonderful, which it was not. His favorite shirt, which he wore all the time, said I'M NUMBER 1 on the front of it. He was more like number 1,000,000,000,000,000,000, but I don't think all those zeros would fit on it.

And then before anyone could ask any more questions I gave my Graces the secret signal, and all together we said, "Start your posters now!" I was tired and super glad to sit down back at my desk. It's a lot harder to be a teacher than a student. Now I could understand why Mr. Frank was having so many troubles with it.

SO FAR SO GOOD

Mr. Frank let everyone work on the posters until it was time for recess. And the only person who said anything in that whole entire time was Miss Lois. She asked us if it was okay to draw a picture on the poster if we wanted. Of course we three Graces all said okay, because it was an excellent idea. And I was really surprised that such a good idea about drawing was coming from Miss Lois. This whole time I thought she only liked words.

At recess time we stayed to help Mr. Frank put up all the finished posters, and when everyone came back to the class after recess, you could tell that they all thought the posters looked amazing, which they did.

MORE PROJECTS

It was really hard to keep concentrating on the other projects because I was trying to read the posters instead. I just couldn't help it. Mr. Frank must have noticed other people doing it too because he interrupted Gary, Sunni, and Margaret, who were in the middle of their project, and said, "As soon as this next group is finished, everyone will have twenty minutes to walk around the class to look at the Lost posters and put notes in the boxes."

Their project was about changing nouns in the Three Bears story and then reading it to us. It was kind of funny because they changed the bears into princesses and the porridge into silly foods like lollipops, worm soup, and cupcakes. You could tell which parts Gary had helped with because Sunni and Margaret are not the kind of girls who like disgusting things. After their story we finally got to go around and read the posters.

MY FAVORITE POSTERS

I liked this one because I could tell that Miss Lois made it. No kids drink coffee, plus I recognized her handwriting. It was proof that she for sure liked our project. At first I was surprised that she likes elephants so much, but then I remembered that she once said she would like to ride on an elephant. It made me wonder if Miss Lois's house was filled with elephant stuff.

WHAT MIGHT BE IN MISS LOIS'S HOUSE

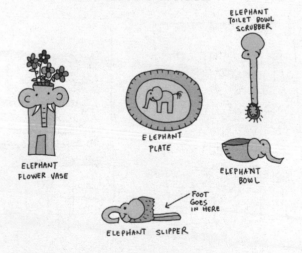

ELEPHANT
TOILET BOWL
SCRUBBER

ELEPHANT
PLATE

ELEPHANT
FLOWER VASE

ELEPHANT
BOWL

FOOT
GOES
IN HERE

ELEPHANT SLIPPER

LOST

MY FAVORITE RED PEN WITH A LIGHT UP STAR ON TOP OF IT.

LOST

my secret ~~trick~~ trick because my brother told what it was to my mom and now she knows so I can't trick her anymore, if I don't eat my peas.

LOST

MY SHIRT FROM CANADA WHICH IS TOO SMALL SO MOM GAVE IT AWAY EVEN IF IT WAS MY FAVORITE!

LOST

my plant because I forgot to give it water and then it died and it was too late to save it even with tons of water.

I wrote notes for five of the posters and then put them in the right numbered box. Mr. Frank was not going to get in trouble this time, I could tell. He was smiling a big smile at Miss Lois, and she was smiling right back at him.

THESE WERE MY NOTES BACK

SORRY ABOUT YOUR CUP.
YOU SHOULD BUY A NEW ONE.
MR. FRANK IS DOING A
REAL GOOD JOB!

OWEN HAS A PEN LIKE
THAT MAYBE HE FOUND
YOURS.

I WOULD LIKE TO KNOW
YOUR SECRET TRICK
BECAUSE I DON'T LIKE PEAS.

I DON'T LIKE WHEN I
GET TOO BIG FOR MY
FAVORITE CLOTHES!

MY MOM ALWAYS KILLS
PLANTS TOO. SHE SAYS
SHE DOESN'T HAVE A
GREEN THUMB MAYBE YOU
DON'T EITHER

WHAT HAPPENED AT LUNCHTIME

I tried to find Mimi so I could tell her that she was the most excellent human *N* I had ever seen, but the Graces found me first and wanted to talk about our project. I was sharing their joy 100 percent, so it was nice to all have lunch together.

MORE AND MORE PROJECTS

There is one thing that I know for sure, and that thing is that I am going to know everything about nouns and other sentence parts and language when these projects are over.

We listened to two more groups and then Mr. Frank gave us another ten minutes to look at the posters one last time. I don't know how I missed it before, but hanging next to the fire alarm was the most saddest Lost poster ever.

It reminded me of how I was feeling when Mimi had her new friend Max following her everywhere so I had to for sure write a note to help this person feel better.

I had to use both sides of the little paper.

THEN FINALLY WE GOT TO OPEN OUR BOXES

Mr. Frank said we could open our boxes at the end of the day. I was super glad about that, because I was crazy with waiting to see what was inside. I was hoping he wasn't going to make us wait until every single project was finished, because that for sure was going to probably take a week. A week is a long time to be looking at a box and wondering what's inside. That kind of waiting can make you have a hard time with concentrating on anything else, which is the exact kind of thing that makes a teacher angry. I sure hoped Miss Lois was paying attention to how Mr. Frank was making all the right decisions with his teaching.

IN MY BOX

There were six notes in my box, which means every single little rip-off note got used, and they were all good except for one. If I didn't know the Big Meanie wasn't really a Big Meanie anymore I would have guessed that the bad note was maybe from her, but because I know her now I could tell that it wasn't. So somewhere in the class there was another meanie, but that didn't matter so much because all the other notes were so perfect, especially the one from Mr. Frank, even though he signed his name and didn't keep it a secret. Plus I could tell that the new meanie was only really a mini meanie anyway, and probably just jealous. Still, I kind of wondered who it was.

NOTES THAT WERE IN MY BOX (NUMBER 11)

I LIKE YOUR NAME EVEN THOUGH THERE ARE 4 OF YOU IN THIS CLASS. [11]

Don't worry Your Real name will always be the Grace one, not the Just Grace one. [11]

You'll ~~be~~ Still Just GRACE FOREVER! 🟦

I WANTED To CALL MY HAMSTER GRACE BUT THEN IT TURNED OUT TO BE A BOY HAMSTER 🟦

Dear Grace, I promise to call you only "Grace" whenever I see you outside the class. SIGNED MR. Frank 🟦

excellent project! You are so smart! 🟦

WHAT HAPPENED WHEN THE BELL RANG AT THE END OF THE DAY

Grace came up to me and said that she thought Mr. Frank was for sure going to get a real good mark on this project from Miss Lois. She could tell this because Mr. Frank and Miss Lois were talking and doing lots of smiling. Then Grace gave me a hug and said, "I'll see you later, Grace." "See you, Grace," I said, and I waved a goodbye at her that turned into a hello wave to Mimi, who was watching us.

Mimi walked over real slow, and that was probably because she was scared she was still going to be allergic to me. I couldn't wait to tell her how great she was in the N, and how I never could have believed it if I didn't see it with my very own eyes.

Mimi was not as happy as I thought she'd be, and I could tell that because of my empathy power. She said thank you but then didn't want to talk about it anymore. I was hoping she would do a handstand just for me so I could see close up how to do it, but instead she wanted to talk about her poster. "Did you guess which one I did?" asked Mimi.

I looked around the room but I couldn't

decide which one to pick. "That one," said Mimi, and she pointed to the Lost My Best Friend poster next to the fire alarm. I couldn't believe it. Mimi had the saddest poster in the whole class and it was a message all about me.

"Mimi, I'm not lost. I'm right here," I said. "But what about your new Grace friends?" asked Mimi. I could tell that she wasn't believing me 100 percent that she was still my best friend forever. She was feeling the exact same way I used to be feeling about Max and Sammy, except maybe even worse, because I didn't make my poster about it.

MY SECRET HELPER

Sometimes it is really hard to make a person believe something when they think another thing might really be the truth. Like how Mimi was thinking that maybe I wanted to be best friends with the Graces instead of her, which was 100 percent not the truth. And if this kind of thing happened, then you could be wishing that you had a real magic bead-head necklace to make a wish on so the not-the-truth feeling would go away.

But I didn't need that because I had something better, and as soon as I showed it to Mimi she knew that we were still the best friends ever. And when we hugged she didn't even have one sneeze!

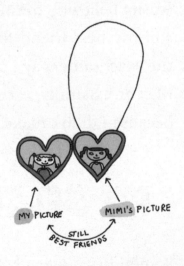

MY PICTURE

MIMI'S PICTURE

STILL BEST FRIENDS

EPILOGUE

I know about the word *epilogue* because sometimes at the last part of an *Unlikely Heroes* show they put it on the TV screen right before they tell you what the people in the story are doing now. Usually it's not hero stuff, but still, it's kind of fun to know about it. An epilogue is the place where you tell what happened at the end, when the main part of the story is finished. Stuff like how I showed Mimi the note I had written about her Lost poster and how that made her smile a real happy Mimi smile. How Owen gave the red pen he had found back to Sarah, who had lost it. How Mr. Frank was for sure going to get an excellent student-teacher mark because now he and Miss Lois smiled at each other all the time and his face never got red. How standing talking to three other Graces at the same time can be really fun. And then, finally, how playing with four friends can sometimes be just as much fun as playing with just one friend, even when that one friend is your best friend forever.

WHAT GRACE WILL BE THINKING ABOUT IN HER NEXT BOOK

Just Grace
Walks the Dog

For the great
dogs I have loved

Mika and Emma

UNFORTUNATE THINGS

There are two kinds of unfortunate things: those that are unfortunate because they have not happened, and those that are unfortunate because they already really did happen. I am pretty unlucky, because right now in my life I have both kinds of unfortunate things happening at the exact same time! My unfortunate thing that did not happen is that I am not allowed to have a dog, and my unfortunate thing that did happen is that at school everyone calls me Just Grace.

Some people say that when bad stuff happens in your life it gives you lots of character, which means that you end up being a super-interesting person when you grow up. I must be filling up with character pretty fast, because unfortunate stuff is always especially happening to me. Maybe that means I'll be on TV or something when I get big.

UNFORTUNATE ON PURPOSE AND UNFORTUNATE MISTAKE

When something unfortunate happens it is probably better if the unfortunate thing is a mistake instead of an on-purpose unfortunate thing. So I am at least lucky about that, because my biggest unfortunate thing was definitely 100 percent an accident.

UNFORTUNATE ON-PURPOSE THING

UNFORTUNATE MISTAKE THING

MY UNFORTUNATE THING

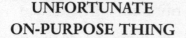

My real name is Grace, but at school my name is Just Grace, which is an unusual, stupid, and completely dumb name. How something can change from nothing special to completely dumb is a long, unfortunate story, and one that I am very tired of explaining. But if I don't explain it, then people think that it's an on-purpose thing and that my parents were crazy to name me that, and that I have been living with the awful Just Grace name since the day I was born, and maybe even worse, that I actually like it. And then they will look at me like I am 100 percent Just Grace. So I have to tell them the story so they can know that only my outside is Just Grace and that on my insides I'm a solid Grace all the way through. It's like being a girl M&M. I look like Just Grace/candy on the outside, but on the inside I'm all Grace/chocolate! It might not seem like it, but it makes a big difference!

CANDY M&M

GIRL M&M

HOW THIS UNFORTUNATE THING HAPPENED

There are four girls named Grace in my class. Miss Lois, my teacher, said that we all had to change our names or she would never be able to get the right Grace's attention when she said "Grace." Even when she was explaining this I could kind of tell she was right because all four of us looked up when she said Grace, and Peter Marchelli, who sits right next to me, didn't even stop doodling on his desk. Miss Lois named Grace Wallace "Grace W.," and Grace Francis "Grace F.," and Grace Landowski "Gracie," and then right before she got to me I said, "Well, if everyone else is having a new name, can I be called just Grace?" Since no one else was using the

Grace name, it seemed like maybe I could have it. But Miss Lois didn't understand me, and even when I tried to tell her about her mistake she still didn't listen, or even care about it anymore. She closed her ears and wrote Just Grace in her rule book of class names and attendance.

ONCE SOMETHING IS WRITTEN IN THIS BOOK IT CAN NEVER BE CHANGED, EVEN IF IT IS WRITTEN IN PENCIL!

And then suddenly it was school law forever, that my new dumb name was Just Grace, because once it is written in the book it can never be changed.

The first person to make fun of me was Grace F., and that was no surprise because back then she was still the Big Meanie and I thought she hated me.

But that was before she changed back into Grace F., who is really very funny and an excellent artist, which are two things you would not imagine could be true until you got to know her.

THREE GRACES PLUS ONE

Grace F., Grace W., and I all had to do a project together, and that is how we all became friends. Grace L. was in another group so she got to be friends with Walker Marcie and Bethany, but I still think it made her sad that she was not friends with us, because our names were all Grace and she was a Grace too, but not one who was in our group. I can figure out stuff like that because of my teeny tiny superpower. My superpower helps me know when people are unhappy, even if they are pretending to be happy, and even if they are very good actors. It's called empathy power. The hard thing about superpowers is that they don't come with an instruction book so it's not always easy to know exactly when and how to use them. I think other superpowers, like

SUPERSTRENGTH POWER—EASY

EMPATHY POWER—NOT EASY

superstrength or x-ray eyes, would be a lot easier to work.

I felt sorry for Grace L. when we other Graces were joking around and having so much fun calling each other Grace, Grace, and Grace. But I couldn't figure out what to do to help her, so I pretended I didn't notice she was sad. This is a very hard thing for a person with my superpower to do, and it can sometimes end up giving me a stomachache.

IF I IGNORE MY SUPERPOWER, I FEEL SICK FOR A LITTLE WHILE.

MR. FRANK

Today was the last day I will ever see Mr. Frank standing in my classroom at school. He was our student teacher and the real reason I became friends with Grace W. and Grace F., who used to be the Big Meanie. He made me work with them when we had to do a language project. Sometimes when someone forces you to do something you would not normally do, the ending part and how it works out is a surprise, one that you would have never guessed in a million years. I would have never thought that I would be friends with or even like the Big Meanie. But I was lucky, because this forcing thing only sometimes works out in a good way.

Dad had to work on a project with a man named Jeremy at his job, and now he says he doesn't like the Jeremy man very much anymore. Before Dad knew him better he thought Jeremy was funny and a hard worker, but now he says Jeremy takes too many coffee breaks and is irresponsible, which is a word I was happy he was using about someone else and not me.

Anytime I do something wrong Dad loves to use the *irresponsible* word on me, and usually he likes to use it more than once or twice in a row.

IT IS IRRESPONSIBLE TO
LEAVE JAM OUTSIDE ON THE
PICNIC TABLE BECAUSE IT
WILL SOON BE FILLED UP WITH
ANTS AND THEN WE WILL HAVE
TO THROW IT IN THE GARBAGE.

THREE NEW THINGS

It was not hard to say goodbye to Mr. Frank.
I did not cry like Jane Dublin did. She will
probably never see him again, so I can understand why she was so sad she had to cry. He
has to go back to the university to finish off
all his learning before he can get his certifi-
cate that says he is a real teacher. Before he
came to our school I didn't know it took so
much work just to stand in front of our class
and tell us what to do. The real reason I did

not cry or feel bad about Mr. Frank leaving is that Grace F. lives right next door to him. She says I can come over to her house anytime I want to see Mr. Frank. And even though her mom won't let us knock on his door, because that would be bothering him, we can probably still see him because she says he usually comes outside if he hears you talking to his dog through the fence. He has a very fat and very friendly golden retriever named Winkie.

I am definitely going to visit Grace F., because one visit to her house will give me three new things all at the same time. I will get to see her bedroom, I will get to call Mr. Frank "Jeffrey," the way she does when he is not in school, and I will get to play with Winkie, his golden retriever. I am newly crazy about dogs. They are like cats, which I already liked, but better because you can take them places with you like a real friend. Plus you can teach them to do tricks and they will try to learn them, which cats definitely don't do.

MIMI

Mimi is my best friend in the whole world and she lives right next door to me. This is extra lucky because stuff like that hardly ever happens. The even better part is that we can see each other from our bedroom windows. Mimi got a book from the library so we could learn Morse code and send flashlight messages to each other at night in the dark. We have tried to do it a couple of times but it's kind of hard and it takes a really long time. I think it's much easier to send the message to Mimi than to figure out the message that she is sending to me. Still, it's a good idea, and if we keep practicing we might get really good at it. It would be excellent to stay up all night flashlight talking. And the extra best part is that none of our parents would ever even know about it.

COVER OF MORSE CODE BOOK

HOW TO DO FLASHLIGHT MORSE CODE

Flashlight Morse code is not fun and easy like it said it was going to be on the cover of Mimi's book. Flashlight Morse code is confusing and frustrating, but they couldn't put that on the cover because then no one would try it. Every letter of the alphabet has a different code, and it's all dots and lines. You have to spell out everything you want to say letter by letter using the right code. A dot means you flash the flashlight on and off really fast, and a dash means you leave the flashlight on for longer. Just to spell out "hi" you have to do four fast flashes for the *h* and then two fast flashes for the *i*. Mimi and I both copied out the code chart and taped it to our windows, but it's still not easy to do. Mimi said the easy part was a lie, but she was sure the fun part would be true if we practiced more.

MORSE CODE CHART

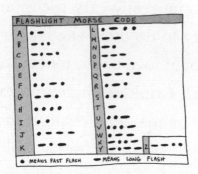

MIMI AND CATS

Mimi is allergic to cats, which is why they used to be my favorite animal and why they are not now. Mrs. Luther, my other next-door neighbor, has a great cat named Crinkles. She says he is a cat-dog, which means she thinks he is kind of like an M&M

too, cat coating on the outside and mostly dog on the inside. I don't think she is really right about that, though. I have tried to teach Crinkles some really easy tricks, and he did not even try to do them at all. If he was part dog, he would love to learn new stuff. Every time I touch Crinkles I have to remember to wash my hands and change my clothes before I see Mimi, or else she will start her sneezing. So it is much easier to just not touch him instead. Mimi is worth it.

MIMI AND DOGS

I thought I would forever not have an animal friend in my life until Mimi said that she thought she might not be allergic to dogs. She went to visit her uncle, and his new dog, Chesapeake, did not make her sneeze even once. And even though she didn't touch him, this was a big surprise, because if she even stands next to a cat she will sneeze like crazy and then have to take her medicine so her eyes don't get puffed up like supersize marshmallows.

SO PUFFY SHE CAN HARDLY OPEN THEM.

SHE SAYS THEY ARE SUPER ITCHY TOO!

MIMI WITH NORMAL EYES

MIMI WITH PUFFED-UP EYES

Mimi is also not allergic to frogs, lizards, snakes, turtles, birds, and fish, but those are not animals that I would want for a pet. I like animals with fur who are cuddly and can make you feel better just by hugging them.

I asked Mom and Dad if I could have a dog and they said no and that to have a dog you have to be dependable and responsible. *Responsible* is the opposite of *irresponsible,* so it is no surprise that Dad thought of that part. *Responsible* and *dependable* are a lot alike, so I made up a chart to show how a good pet owner like me would behave to be both. And then so Mom and Dad could know that I was being serious, I taped it to the fridge. We have one of those fridges that look magnetic but then when you put a magnet on them the magnet just falls off. That means we have to tape everything on, which is much uglier, plus we don't get to use cute or funny magnets like most other people do.

DEPENDABLE	RESPONSIBLE
- FEED DOG 2 TIMES A DAY.	- COME HOME RIGHT AFTER SCHOOL TO LET DOG OUT.
- TAKE DOG OUT FOR WALKS EVERY DAY.	- MAKE SURE DOG'S FEET ARE NOT MUDDY.
- BRUSH DOG'S FUR.	- DO NOT LET DOG EAT GARBAGE.
- GIVE DOG WATER SO HE DOES NOT DRINK OUT OF THE TOILET.	- TAKE DOG TO THE DOCTOR IF HE IS SICK.
- LOVE DOG EVERY DAY.	

MIMI TEST

Mimi and I decided to go to the park to test for sure that she is not allergic to dogs. There are always dogs in the park, so it was easy. We stayed for over an hour and played with three little dogs and two big dogs, and

Mimi did not even have one single sneeze the whole time. It was amazing! She even let one of the dogs lick her chin. I was worried about that because that was awful close to her eyes, and you really aren't supposed to let strange dogs lick your face. I think she was just so excited to be close to a friendly, furry animal that she couldn't help it. It was hard to get Mimi to leave since she has been starved of animal attention her whole entire life. When something super good is happening, it is hard to give it up and just go home. We talked all the way home about how we

MIMI WITH REAL DOG

couldn't believe all the time we had wasted when we could have had a dog in our lives. And how that was going to have to change really soon.

ANIMAL PEOPLE

Mimi is not allowed to have a dog because her parents are not animal people. Her mom and dad did not have any pets when they were growing up, so they can't really help the way they are. It is very hard to change a non–animal person into an animal person. My mom and dad both had pets when they were kids so they have to be animal people, even though when I asked them they said they are not. They probably wouldn't admit it but they are sort of like M&M's too. They have non–animal person outsides with ani-

mal person insides. All I have to do is peel off
their outside non–animal person shells.

MOM AND DAD

SHELL ON   **SHELL OFF**

DOG CHOICES

Mimi says that she is more of a big-dog person than a little-dog person. I don't know
how she can know that, because up until we
went to the park she didn't know if she was
even an any-kind-of-dog person. At first I

thought it was maybe because little dogs reminded her of cats and her allergies, but she said it wasn't that. Now I think it's because she is so excited about dogs that she wants to have as much dog as she can get. It's like if you suddenly tasted ice cream for the first time in your life and found out you totally loved it. You'd want to eat the whole container. I told Mimi that I think our chances of being allowed to have a dog are better if we pick a little dog, because a little dog is closer to a no dog than a big dog is.

MAX

Max is Mimi's next-door neighbor. He is my one-house-away neighbor. He and Mimi and Sammy Stringer did their school project together, which is how they all became friends. Sammy spends a lot of time visiting with Max. Sometimes Mimi and I do stuff with them, because if they are right there standing outside it's not polite to ignore them.

Sammy is not my favorite person, but I am starting to like him a little better. Mom says your tastes change when you grow up, so I guess that is what's happening. So far I still don't like grapefruits or cabbage or peas or spinach, so the food-tastes-changing part probably hasn't started yet. When Mom was little she said she didn't like potatoes or tomatoes, but now that she is grown up she loves them. I hope she is  wrong about the food-tastes-changing part, because I can't imagine eating a cabbage and saying "yummy" at the same time. That would be disgusting!

PICKING A DOG

Max came over when Mimi and I were standing outside talking about the kinds of dogs we liked. "German shepherds are the best dogs ever," said Max. "My uncle has one, and Lady can do all sorts of tricks and even lets you use her tummy as a pillow when you want to take a nap." "Oh my gosh! That sounds perfect!" said Mimi. "I think we should get a German shepherd!" "Wow! Are you getting a dog?" asked Max. "I could teach it some tricks." Talking to Max was not helping Mimi to change her mind and forget about picking a big dog. So I said, "Isn't a German shepherd the same kind of dog that Mr. Hurley has?" Mr. Hurley is our neighbor across the street, and his dog, Oliver, who is a German shepherd, is not even a teeny tiny one bit friendly. He acts like he can't wait to get away from you, and Mr. Hurley always says, "Leave him be, children. He's not used to you little ones." Even though none of us is really that little anymore.

"Yeah, well, that's because he's seventy-seven years old," said Max. "Mr. Hurley is that old?" I was surprised. Mr. Hurley looked old, but old like my dad, not old like a grandpa. "No, not him, silly—Oliver." Now Max was laughing at me. "Oliver is seventy-seven dog years old, which is eleven years old in human years." Sometimes Max thinks he is such a smarty-pants and the knower of everything about everything. I was glad when Mimi said, "I don't know—Oliver doesn't seem like he was ever very friendly. And his fur doesn't look very soft either." We would have probably talked about it some more, but Sammy walked up and Sammy is not a furry-animal person. Not on the outside or on the inside.

DID YOU KNOW THAT 1 HUMAN YEAR IS EQUAL TO 7 DOG YEARS?

OF COURSE I CAN'T COUNT, BECAUSE I'M A DOG.

RESPONSIBLE AND DEPENDABLE

Mom and Dad said that it takes much more than making a list to prove that you are responsible and dependable. Then they told me all the kinds of things that dog owners have to do. I knew about most of them already, but not the part about having to clip the dog's toenails. It sounded kind of gross and hard to do, but I pretended I already knew all about it. Of course Dad also talked about having to pick up the poop. Nobody likes that part, but I bet if I wore rubber gloves and didn't breathe through my nose I could do it. It's the only really yucky thing about having a dog.

Then, while my brain was still thinking about everything, Dad said, "Maybe we can talk about it again when you are older." He always says this when I ask about something fun that he doesn't want me to have. When I'm older I'm going to be so busy with all the fun things I don't get to do now that I won't even have time to do my homework, and it will be all his fault!

I went up to my room to be mad all alone and draw a comic. Sometimes when I am feeling bad it helps me if I draw something.

NOW THAT I'M OLDER

MISS LOIS

Miss Lois is my teacher at school, and I used to not really like her very much, but that was mostly because I didn't understand her yet. It's like the thing that happened with liking the Big Meanie better, only Miss Lois is a grownup and she never stuck her tongue out at me. Now that Mr. Frank is gone, Miss Lois is going to be our only teacher again. I didn't even try to ask her about changing my Just Grace name, because she would have for sure said no. In Miss Lois's head, right next to her great love of elephants, because that is her favorite animal, is my Just Grace name. And just like an elephant, she is never going to forget it. Elephants are supposed to have amazing memories, so that is too bad for me.

MISS LOIS THINKING

MISS LOIS'S NEW PROJECT

Miss Lois wants us all to keep a journal and to write in it every day for a whole week. She gave everyone in the class a special red notebook to use for the project. She said she is not going to share what we write with the rest of the class, so we can write about stuff that is sort of private if we want to, but that we should remember that *she* is going to read it to make sure we did everything like we were supposed to. I guess she doesn't want us to be embarrassed about what we write down.

Miss Lois said it's easy to keep a journal if you pick the same time to work on it each day. That way you won't forget about writing in it and miss days, and then have to make up a bunch of stuff at the last minute before you have to hand it in. She also said we could use drawings and photos if we wanted, which is great, because I love to make both of those things. Before I knew Miss Lois better I didn't think she liked pictures, so it was a big happy surprise to find out that she likes to draw. We have to write at least four sentences every day, and they can't be the same four sentences over and over. I know that because Drake Brooks said, "I eat waffles for breakfast every morning—can I just write that each day?"

THIS BOOK BELONGS TO

EVERYONE
HAD TO WRITE
THEIR NAME HERE.
OF COURSE I HAD
TO WRITE JUST GRACE

THE RED NOTEBOOK

WHAT IS GOOD ABOUT WRITING IN A JOURNAL

Miss Lois said that writing in a journal every day is rewarding and it shows commitment. The rewarding part is that when you get older you can look back and see what you were thinking and doing when you were young, because she said we are all going to do lots of forgetting as we get older and we won't remember everything we are doing right now. The commitment part shows that you are dedicated and dependable.

As soon as Miss Lois said *dependable* it made me a lot more excited about the project. When I was finished I was going to show it to Dad and he would have to cross the dependable part off of my list of stuff I have to prove to him. Then all I would have to do was find something for the responsible part. I couldn't wait to tell Mimi we were closer to a dog already.

After school Mimi and I did some more dog talking, and even though we are both excited about dogs, we are not excited about the same dog. Mimi is not giving up on her love for a big dog, and I am not giving up on my love for a little dog. This means we have a big problem. Being best friends does not always mean you like the same things every single time. Sometimes it would be 100 percent easier if this was true.

BIG DOG VERSUS LITTLE DOG

THE BEST SHOW IN THE WORLD

Instead of fighting about dogs, we decided to go and watch an episode of *Unlikely Heroes*. This is our most favorite show in the whole world. Every week they show you different real normal people who have done super-hero-type things.

Last week there was a man who jumped in front of a car to save a runaway baby stroller from getting hit. The car hit the man and he went flying over the top of it and landed right on the roof of the car behind. Except for a sprained finger, he wasn't even hurt. This was a good thing, because there wasn't a baby in the stroller and if the man had been hurt for nothing that would have been really sad. Everybody at the accident said the man was a hero anyway, and I guess that made him happy because he was smiling a lot when the show's hosts were interviewing him.

Max came outside just as we were walking up Mimi's steps, so we asked him if he wanted to watch the show with us. Max loves *Unlikely Heroes* too, but that is only because we told him so much about it. Before he moved next door to Mimi he hadn't even really watched it.

YOU'RE RIGHT! THIS SHOW IS AMAZING!

HOW TO SOLVE A PROBLEM

Before the show started Mimi and I had to argue about big dogs and little dogs a little more—we couldn't help it. It surprised me

100 percent, but Max came up with a way so that we would never fight about dogs again. He said we should make a chart of all the dogs we met and write down everything that was good and bad about each one. Then at the end we could go down the list and pick the best dog. It was such a perfect way for us to decide on our dog. I couldn't believe that I didn't think of it. I almost didn't want to watch the show, I was so excited about getting started. But I did anyway because when you love something as much as I love *Unlikely Heroes,* you just can't say no, especially if it is a new episode that you haven't seen before.

UNLIKELY HEROES SHOW

AND THEN I GRABBED HER ARM.

WOW

MAN TALKING ABOUT HOW HE SAVED HIS MOM FROM FALLING OFF A BOAT WHEN SHE TRIPPED. IT WAS A CRUISE SHIP-TYPE BOAT.

TV SET

REALLY AMAZING BECAUSE HE IS IN A WHEELCHAIR.

THE DOG LIST

After the show, Max wanted to teach us how to do cartwheels, but we were too excited to work on our dog list to learn. Max loves to teach people to do new things, so he was disappointed that we were not in love with his cartwheel idea. I knew he was sad, so I said, "When we get a dog, you can teach it to do a flip." This made him happy and he said he was going to go home and look up dog tricks on his computer.

I didn't say anything about it, but I think it is a lot easier to teach a little dog to do a flip than a big dog. I don't even know if big dogs can do flips.

When he was gone, Mimi and I got started on a chart. We hadn't met any dogs yet so we just made a list of little and big dog things. The first things we wrote down were the good and the bad about each kind of dog.

BIG   LITTLE

BIG DOG GOOD	BIG DOG BAD	LITTLE DOG GOOD	LITTLE DOG BAD
① CAN USE DOG AS A PILLOW.	① LOTS OF FUR EVERYWHERE.	① CAN CARRY DOG IF HE GETS TIRED.	① TOO SMALL TO BE COZY WITH.
② CAN PROTECT YOU.	② BIG POOPS.	② SMALL POOPS.	② NOT AS MUCH DOG TO LOVE.
③ MORE DOG TO LOVE.	③ MAKES MORE MESS.	③ DOES NOT GET IN THE WAY.	③ LITTLE DOGS BARK MORE.
④ NICE-SOUNDING BARK.	④ HARDER TO GIVE A BATH TO.	④ CAN SIT IN YOUR LAP	④ YAPPY BARK.
⑤ CAN SWIM.	⑤ TAKES UP MORE OF YOUR BED.	⑤ NOT AS MUCH FUR.	⑤ LOTS OF LITTLE DOGS DON'T SWIM.

Mimi had some really good big-dog reasons, but still my mind was not changed. I don't think she liked my number-two reason about why little dogs were better. But it was something that was true, so she couldn't take it off the list. The only person who would maybe even be excited about the number-two reason at all was Sammy Stringer. He once did a whole photo project where he just took pictures of dog poop. When someone does something like that it is hard to forget it, even if you are starting to think he is maybe an okay person after all.

MY JOURNAL

I started on my journal writing, and it was surprisingly easy to write four sentences. One of my sentences was even super long because I had so much to put in it. I cannot believe that some of the kids in my class were complaining about having to do journal writing. I am going to work on my journal every night after dinner when there is nothing else going on. When there is daylight, too much stuff is happening, and that makes it a lot harder to concentrate.

Mimi is my best friend in the whole world, though right now we are not getting along 100 percent. We are trying to pick a dog and we both want something different. I want a little dog because they are cuter and I think that Mom and Dad would maybe say yes to a small dog because then they wouldn't notice it so much. Mimi wants a big dog because she thinks they are cozier and you can use their bodies as a pillow.

AUGUSTINE DUPRE

Augustine Dupre is my grown-up French friend.

HELLO

BONJOUR

SHE HAS ONE FOOT IN THE U.S.A.

AND

SHE HAS ONE FOOT IN FRANCE

She is a flight attendant, and she lives in the fancy apartment that Dad made in our basement. There are lots of great things about Augustine Dupre, but the best thing is that she is a great listener when you have a problem you want to talk about. If you don't have a problem, then she is still fun and interesting to talk to, because she is full of amazing stories about her trips to France. She

goes to France almost
every week.

Mom doesn't like
me going downstairs
to the basement at
night to talk to her.
She says, "Augustine is
probably tired from all
her traveling, and I'm

**AUGUSTINE DUPRE
IN HER FLIGHT
ATTENDANT
UNIFORM**

sure she does not have the energy to talk to
an eight-year-old." Sometimes Mom just says
the silliest things, because anyone knows it
hardly takes up any energy at all to just talk.

IT'S OKAY TO BE SNEAKY IF YOU DON'T GET CAUGHT

When Mom was busy in the kitchen I snuck
downstairs and knocked on Augustine
Dupre's door. I have a special knock so she

knows it's me—that way she doesn't have to shoo Crinkles out the window if he is visiting her. Crinkles loves Augustine Dupre, maybe even more than he loves Mrs. Luther, who is his owner. They both buy him treats, and you can tell it just by looking at him, because he is getting kind of fat. Augustine Dupre is not allowed to have any pets in her apartment, so when Crinkles is visiting her we have to keep it a secret. Dad made this rule while he was wearing his non–animal person outside shell. Once we get a dog he'll change his mind about Crinkles for sure.

Of course Augustine Dupre is an animal person, and it turns out that she is not just a cat person, but a dog person too. She loved my idea about getting a dog to share with Mimi. It's a good thing that Crinkles does not really understand people talk, because he would not have been so happily sitting on

Augustine Dupre's lap if he knew we were trying to bring a dog into our lives. Some cats can kind of like dogs, but Crinkles does not look like that kind of cat.

CRINKLES MEETING A DOG

AUGUSTINE DUPRE'S IDEA

Augustine Dupre said that I had to show my parents that I was capable of taking care of a dog. *Capable* was her word, and since it seemed like it kind of meant the same sort of thing as *dependable*, it sounded like a good idea. *Capable* means you are able to do a certain thing, and the certain thing I had to do was to take care of a dog. This is not an easy thing to show someone you can do if you don't have a real dog to do it with. Augustine Dupre said there is a real difference between the saying you can do something and actually really doing the something.

HOW SHE GAVE ME HER IDEA

Sometimes when Augustine Dupre has an idea in her head she doesn't tell you in words what that idea is—instead, she likes to give you lots of hints. And then after enough hints, suddenly you know what she is talking about because her idea pops right into your head.

I could tell that she was doing this because I wanted to talk about dogs and she wanted to talk about other things. Usually she is happy to mostly talk about whatever I want to talk about. But this time she wanted to talk about the Crinkles postcard project that I made for Mrs. Luther and all the boxes I put together for the Lost poster project.

Then just before I was about to leave she said, "Yes, it's too bad you don't have some kind of dog so you could show your parents how you would care for it." I was feeling sad because this was true, but then just two seconds later Augustine Dupre's idea popped right into my head.

I was so excited, I shouted the idea out loud. "Wonderful!" said Augustine Dupre. "You are so clever." And then she gave me a big hug. Augustine Dupre always pretends the idea is 100 percent my idea, even if she did lots of helping to get me to think of it. I think she would be a very good teacher. Usually I don't like to leave her apartment, but this was not the way I was feeling with the new big idea in my head. I couldn't wait to get upstairs so I could tell Mimi about it.

PHONE RULES

Mom has a rule about no starting phone calls after 8:00 p.m., so I couldn't call Mimi because it was already 8:10. If only I had figured out the big idea ten minutes earlier, everything would have been perfect. I'm actually allowed to talk on the phone until 8:15 if I started talking before 8:00. It seems like a silly rule, but it works okay. Mimi's mom liked it so much, she made it a rule at her house too. This is good, because it's kind of easier when friends have the same rules about stuff like the phone. I would feel bad if

YOU CAN'T USE ME NOW!

Mimi was allowed to talk until 8:30 and we always had to stop at 8:15 just because of me.

Morse Code Talking

As soon as I got to my room, I started wishing that I had been practicing the Morse code better. It was impossible to tell Mimi the whole dog idea with Morse code because it would take way too many words and that would be way too many flashes. I saw Mimi in her room, but it took forever before I could get her attention. Finally, she noticed me flashing my light at her window. The hard thing about the flashlight Morse code is that you have to do the dot parts really fast so that they don't get confused with the dash parts.

**THIS IS WHAT THE WORDS *DOG IDEA*
LOOK LIKE IN MORSE CODE.**

I had to do it twice because Mimi got confused the first time. I know this because we made up a signal for *confused*. You make big circles with your flashlight. This works out well, because it also sort of helps you feel better when you wave your arm around. I think it kind of gets the mad feelings out. It's too bad it's not the kind of thing you could do if you were mad and not in your room, because people would for sure think that you were crazy.

BREAKFAST

Mimi came over extra early at breakfast time because she wanted to know why I didn't want to get a dog anymore. She got the Morse code wrong and thought I had spelled out *nog idea* instead of *dog idea* like I really had. The *n* and the *d* are kind of close when you are using Morse code, and she had not seen one of my fast flashes.

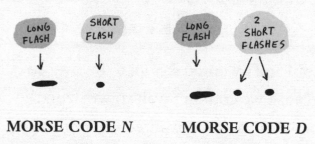

MORSE CODE *N*   **MORSE CODE *D***

Mimi said it took her a long time, but she finally decided that *nog* must be short for **n**ot "**o**" **g**ood, and so she thought I was saying *not* *"o" good idea* and was giving up on getting a dog. Mom heard us talking and said, "I sure wish she would give up on it." This was not a good thing. But Mimi was glad to hear that this was not true. On the way to school I told Mimi all about my new dog idea, and together we decided it was absolutely, marvelously brilliant!

SOMETIMES A DAY CAN LAST FOREVER

Mimi and I wanted school to be over so badly, because we couldn't wait to work on the new dog idea. School wanted to punish us for wanting to leave, so it made the day go extra super slow. I know that's not what really happened, but it sure felt like it. I had lunch with my two Graces and Mimi. Mimi and I were going to keep the whole picking-out-a-dog project a secret, but when you are totally 100 percent excited about something it is impossible to not talk about it. So we ended up telling the Graces about our big-dog little-dog list. Grace F. said she was only a little bit of a dog person, and Grace W. said she was a lot of a non–dog person.

GRACE F.

I ONLY LIKE SOME DOGS. I'M PICKY.

I DON'T REALLY LIKE DOGS AT ALL.

GRACE W.

One thing for sure is that you cannot tell if a person is a dog person or a non–dog person by just looking at her. Grace F. said she only liked some dogs, and it was lucky that Mr. Frank's dog, Winkie, was one of them, because it would be no fun to live next door to a dog that you didn't like. She invited both

Mimi and me to come over so we could meet Winkie and put him on our list. I think she felt a little bad that Winkie was a big dog and that she didn't have a wonderful little dog for me to put on the list too. That way both Mimi and I could be even. Mimi said she couldn't wait to meet Winkie and wouldn't it be great if he was the first dog at the top of our list. She was so excited and smiley about it that I had to say yes, even though I wanted to go straight home to work on my dog idea instead. Grace F. said it was okay to come over, so we decided to go to her house right after school. It was kind of on our way home, and I was hoping we'd maybe leave pretty quick—that way we would still have time to work on the dog idea before supper.

MIMI ALREADY BEING IN LOVE

Some Other Things That Happened at School

Miss Lois reminded us all not to forget to write in our journals. When she said that, Peter Marchelli put his hand up to his mouth and said, "Oops." Miss Lois didn't notice, but it was obvious that he had not even started on his journal project yet.

Max told Mimi that on the Internet it said that golden retriever–type dogs are very easy to train. This made Mimi even more excited about meeting Winkie.

Sammy Stringer asked me if it was true that I was getting a dog. When I said yes, he said, "But why?" This is not any easy question to answer, because there are all kinds of reasons why, and none of them was going to make any sense to Sammy because he was a non–dog person. So I didn't answer and instead just moved my shoulders up and down in the I-don't-know-why way. I remembered how Sammy had to wear oven mitts when he was going to touch Crinkles, and this made me imagine what his dog-touching outfit would look like.

SAMMY'S DOG-TOUCHNG OUTFIT

I guess I was smiling about it, because he said, "See if I care!" in a mad way and walked off. I think he thought I was making fun of him, which I was not. If you just think about something in your head it does not count as for real, and you are not allowed to get in trouble just for thinking things.

I noticed Grace L. staring at me and Mimi and the other Graces when we were eating lunch.

ONE DOG

If I was a lying type of person I'd say that Winkie is unfriendly, mean, stinky, ugly, and has really hard unsoft-type fur. But I'm not, so I had to write down the truth. He really is a wonderful dog, but he was big not only because he is a golden retriever–type dog, but because he is fat. I just know that Mom and Dad would never let me have a dog like that in our house, and especially not on my bed. He is not the kind of dog you could forget you had because he just kind of blended in with stuff. He is a stick-out dog, a supersizer! I tried to tell Mimi that we couldn't go from being a no-dog house to being a monster-size dog house all at once, but she wouldn't listen.

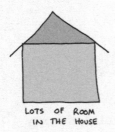

LOTS OF ROOM
IN THE HOUSE

NOT SO MUCH ROOM
IN THE HOUSE BECAUSE
THE DOG IS TAKING UP
SO MUCH SPACE. IT
IS HARD TO NOT NOTICE
THIS DOG.

**NO DOG
IN THE HOUSE**

**MONSTER-SIZE DOG
IN THE HOUSE**

TWO THINGS I DID NOT GET TO DO

At Grace F.'s house we did not see Mr. Frank, so I did not get to call him his not-in-school name of Jeffrey, and we did not get to see

Grace F.'s bedroom. The only part of the visit that worked out like I'd hoped was the leaving-pretty-quick part. Mimi and I got back to my house with lots of time to work on the dog idea before dinner. Mimi's sweatshirt was covered with Winkie's dog hair, but she didn't seem to mind it one little bit. I knew someone with the name of Mom who would not be excited about hair like that all over her house.

The first thing we did, before anything else, was put Winkie on our new dog chart. Max's idea was much better than just a big-dog-versus-little-dog list. After Mimi had written down all the good things about Winkie on the good side of the list, I added my two things to the bad side. Mimi let me draw the picture of Winkie, because drawing is one of the things I like to do more than she does.

NAME OF DOG	GOOD THINGS	BAD THINGS
Winkie Golden retriever type	Friendly, cozy, smart, soft fur, likes to play, gives ball back when playing catch, and can sit if you tell him to.	Loses lots of his fur all over your clothes. Would fill up too much of your house.

MY DOG IDEA

Mimi and I started on the idea as soon as we finished putting Winkie on the chart. It took a lot of cardboard and a lot of tape, but when we were finished we were really happy with how it turned out. The shape of it was just like a real dog. Then, after we painted it, it looked even better. We didn't plan it that way, but it turned out to be a medium-size dog, not big, not little, more just in the middle, and because of that both Mimi and I loved it the same.

OUR PRETEND DOG

HOOK FOR LEASH. WE ARE USING ONE OF MY BELTS.

BEFORE PAINTING   **AFTER PAINTING**

Sometimes the most fun part of a project is the making-stuff part, but this was not true this time. I could hardly wait to show him to Mom and Dad, and then after that to start using him as if he were a real dog. Both Mimi and I decided he was a boy dog and not a girl dog. I don't know why, but he just was. We were going to name him Box Dog, but then Mimi said we should try to think of something cute so my mom and dad would like him better. That was a really good idea for her to think of, and one that was going to help us for sure.

DOG NAMES WE THOUGHT OF

Pepper

Sparky

Spotty

Coffee

(Mimi thought we could name it this because my mom loves coffee so much, but then I reminded her that my dad hates coffee, so we had to do more thinking.)

Pie

We named the box dog Pie (because everybody in my family loves pie), but then after about three minutes I thought of something else even better. I got the idea because Mimi said the name should be something cute, and we wanted it to be something that both Mom and Dad really loved. Sometimes you think you have a great idea and then— surprise!—an even better idea comes along.

When I was little I loved ketchup. I still like it, but I guess back then I had trouble saying the name right. Mom and Dad love to tell the story of how instead of saying "ketchup," I called it "chip-up." Mom says it was one of the cutest things she ever heard. Even now, every time we have ketchup, Mom and Dad talk about the chip-up story. After I told this all to Mimi, she said we definitely had to name our dog Chip-Up. Just doing that was going to help us a ton.

INTRODUCING CHIP-UP

I asked Mom if Mimi could stay for dinner, and of course she said yes. I was a little bit nervous about showing Chip-Up to Mom and Dad, so it was nice to have Mimi there to help. Right before dinner we put a bowl down on the kitchen floor next to Chip-Up so he could have dinner too. It didn't take long for Mom to notice him, and when we told her his name she even made the cute *awww* sound. Dad liked him too. He said Chip-Up looked very well proportioned, which means he thought we did a good job

KETCHUP ON TABLE

CHIP-UP ON FLOOR

making his legs and body and head all the right sizes.

After dinner we took Chip-Up outside to go to the bathroom, because that is the kind of thing a real dog owner would have to do. We were going to take him for a walk, but he didn't slide very well on the sidewalk. I was worried that he would get all ripped up, so I picked him up and carried him. Good thing he wasn't a real dog or he would have been really heavy and probably squirmy too. Chip-Up of course was per-fectly behaved! It was also kind of nice not to have to pick up real dog poop.

**ME CARRYING
CHIP-UP**

JOURNAL TIME AGAIN

After Mimi left I took Chip-Up to my room, but it took a while for me to decide where to put him. Finally I put him on the bed next to me, because that is where a real dog would probably want to go. I put him on his side so he could be more comfy and maybe even sleepy, but he didn't look like either of those things because his legs were sticking out sideways. It looked much more real and better after I covered him up with the quilt that Grandma made me. He was kind of cute, and looked all cozy with just his little head sticking out. It was hard to stop touching and playing with him and concentrate on my journal writing. I wonder if that happens with real dogs too? I wonder if the kids in my class who have real dogs have trouble concentrating and doing their homework? I wonder if they would rather play with their dog instead of write in their journal like they are supposed to?

Today I have a new dog in my life. His name is Chip-Up, and he is the most well-behaved dog in the world. He is going to help Mimi and me get a real dog in our lives. I can tell that my mom and dad are already falling in love with him.

I really, really wanted to take Chip-Up downstairs and introduce him to Augustine Dupre, but there was no way that Mom was not going to notice me when I had a box dog following me down the stairs, so we just stayed in my room. I wonder if real dogs make it hard for you to be sneaky too?

WHAT WE DID BEFORE BED

Chip-Up watched me take a bath, he helped me clean up my room, and then right before bed we both waved good night to Mimi, who was perfectly looking out her window at exactly the right time. I was tired, so I'm glad Mimi wasn't wanting to start any flashlight talking. Flashlight talking is not like regular talking. It takes a lot more of your energy.

ME AND CHIP-UP IN MY BED

WHERE CHIP-UP WAS IN THE MORNING

I bet a real dog would be a lot more cozy to sleep with than Chip-Up was. His edges were pointy, and he was taking up a lot of the bed with his very pokey body. In the middle of the night I had to push him onto the floor. I was glad he wasn't a real dog because I would have felt pretty bad about that if he was. But still I felt a little guilty, so I said, "I'm sorry, Chip-Up," even though he couldn't understand me or care.

SAMMY'S GREAT IDEA

I took Chip-Up outside to go to the bathroom before I even had any of my breakfast. It seemed sort of silly since he really wasn't going to do anything, but like Augustine

Dupre said, it was the showing part that was important. While I was outside standing around, Sammy came by with our newspaper. He used to deliver the paper late, but Max said people were starting to complain, so he is trying harder to be on time. He seemed really happy to see me and Chip-Up, and he stopped his bike right in our driveway.

"Oh, I thought you were getting a real dog," said Sammy. "Did you make him?"

I didn't want to make Sammy nervous, so I didn't say anything about Chip-Up one day turning into a real dog. "Mimi and I did it. His name is, uh . . . Chip-Up." I was surprised, but Sammy was acting like he was really impressed! And then he surprised me even more with a great idea when I wasn't even looking for one.

"You can borrow my skateboard if you want. If you tape his feet to it, you can pull him around with you and stuff."

SAMMY'S SKATEBOARD

Most people in the world would think it was totally weird for a girl to be standing outside on her front grass in her pajamas with a dog made out of boxes, but not Sammy. He liked weird things. Weird things were normal to him. And then for the first time ever in my whole entire life I thought, *Am I weird too?* This is not the best thing to suddenly start thinking about first thing in

the morning, but Sammy didn't notice. "I'll bring the board over to Max's later," said Sammy, and then he rode away.

After our breakfast, mine real and Chip-Up's pretend, we went downstairs to see Augustine Dupre. She answered her door in a fancy red robe that matched her red curtains perfectly, which was no surprise because she always looks excellent. Of course she noticed Chip-Up right away—she is good like that. "I love it! It's perfect!" she said, and then she gave me a hug. As much as Augustine Dupre loved Chip-Up, Crinkles hated Chip-Up. He backed up into the fridge and started growling and hissing and poofed his fur up so he looked even fatter than he really was. I was right about him: Crinkles is 100 percent not a dog-liking cat! I would have stayed longer, but Augustine Dupre said I should probably leave before Crinkles had a heart attack. It was kind of nice to think that Chip-Up looked so good that Crinkles thought he was

real. I was definitely going to tell Mimi about that part.

WHAT HAPPENED AT SCHOOL THAT WAS EXCITING

Nothing.

SCHOOL VERSUS AFTER SCHOOL

1 School is more exciting than after school.

2 School is the same amount of exciting as after school.

3 School and after school are both not exciting.

4 School is less exciting than after school.

When Mr. Frank was our teacher, we had a lot of number 1 and number 2 days. Now with just Miss Lois, we are getting a lot more number 4 days. It would be great if she could put some more of the number 2 days back.

BEFORE THE DOG PARK

Mimi and I couldn't wait to get out of school so we could go to the park and meet some more dogs for our list. Of course Mimi wanted a full report on Chip-Up and everything that had happened after she went home the night before. I think she was a little sad that she couldn't have Chip-Up at her house too, but that was not part of the project. Chip-Up had to stay with me so that Mom and Dad could see my responsibility parts working. When I told her about Sammy Stringer's skateboard idea, she loved it. She wanted to put Chip-Up on the skateboard right away so we could take him to the park with us to meet the other dogs. After school we went to Max's house to get the skateboard, but Sammy hadn't dropped it off yet. Max wanted to see Chip-Up so much that we had to take him to my house to meet him even though we were in a big rush to get to the park. This was a lucky thing because I was totally forgetting about having to take Chip-Up outside to go to the bathroom before we left.

While we were outside, Max tried to throw Chip-Up around like he was doing flips and tricks. I was glad when Mimi got mad and said, "You have to treat Chip-Up like he's a real dog! Would you throw a real dog into the air? I sure hope not!" It's not fun to be with Mimi when she is angry. I guess Max knows that too, because right away he said he was sorry and that he didn't know there were rules about Chip-Up. This was a good thing to do, because Mimi was instantly smiling again and she even invited him to come to the park with us. Chip-Up couldn't come because he didn't have his wheels yet and none of us wanted to carry him all that way. If he was a real dog I am sure he would have been bark-ing and yelping with unhappiness because he was tied to the front porch and was being left behind. Sometimes it was a good thing that he was only made of cardboard.

THE DOG PARK

There were so many dogs at the dog park, we could hardly decide who we should go and meet first, and then by the end we didn't even meet all of them. The owner people thought it was interesting that we were writing down notes, and were extra friendly and helpful about telling us lots of information about their dogs.

My favorite dog of the whole park was a little Jack Russell–type dog named Emma. Even Mimi liked her. She was super cute and super smart. One of her favorite things to do was to chase a soccer ball. If you kicked it she would chase it and bring it right back to you by pushing it with her nose. Max said that that kind of dog can for sure do a flip, because he had seen one do it in a commercial on TV.

When we got home Mimi and I went inside to add all the new dogs to the chart. Max went home to see if the skateboard was there.

DOG CHART PART 2

NAME OF DOG	GOOD THINGS	BAD THINGS
Winkie Golden retriever type	Friendly, cozy, smart, soft fur, likes to play, gives ball back when playing catch, and can sit if you tell him to.	Loses lots of his fur all over your clothes. Would fill up too much of your house.
Emma Jack Russell type	Smart, funny, friendly, cute, and soft	Can't think of one bad thing!
Flash Bulldog type	Mostly liked chewing on sticks. Loved to chase sticks too.	Did not really like the other dogs. Was droolly and looked really heavy.

NAME OF DOG	GOOD THINGS	BAD THINGS
Morgan Cocker spaniel type	Liked the other dogs a lot. Had extra- soft, cozy ears. Chased the ball and mostly brought it back.	Its fur was kind of dirty and its owner said it needed lots of baths and brushing.
Penny Mixed dog	Would chase squirrels out of your yard.	Didn't care about being petted.
Bernie Mixed dog	Was very friendly and liked to play ball and chase the other dogs.	Fur was not super soft.
Oakley Labrador type	Wanted to chase the ball forever.	Did not want to be petted for very long. Did not like other dogs.

NAME OF DOG	GOOD THINGS	BAD THINGS
Cougar Labrador mixed	Loved to be petted and loved watching the other dogs.	Seemed like he was really sleepy because he did a lot of lying down.
Mika German shepherd mix	Was super smart, could even do tricks. Liked people more than dogs.	Can't think of one bad thing except that she was a big dog.

Writing a chart about dogs is a lot of work and a very tiring project, especially if you are the one who still has to draw all the pictures of the dogs at the end of the doing the words part. Mimi was nice and went downstairs to get us a snack from my kitchen while I was doing all the drawing.

She took Chip-Up with her because she said she wanted to do some practicing of taking care of a dog in a house.

When she got back it was almost time for supper, so it was a good thing that Mom did not see her taking the cookies off the counter. Moms don't like it if you eat four or five cookies when there are only about ten minutes until suppertime, even if you are totally and completely 100 percent starving so you would eat all the food on your plate at supper anyway.

I could tell that Mimi was loving Chip-Up because she asked me to put him on my window ledge at night. That way she could see him if she looked at my window from her house. She put him there to show me how perfectly he would fit, but he fell off onto the floor and squished one of his ears. Mimi felt really bad about that and was about to cry until I reminded her to remember that he was only a cardboard dog, so he couldn't really be hurt.

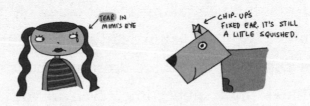

TEAR IN MIMI'S EYE

CHIP-UP'S FIXED EAR. IT'S STILL A LITTLE SQUISHED.

She still told him she was sorry and we tried to fix his ear. Mimi put him on my bed and I put a cover over him so we couldn't see his legs sticking out funny on the side. "He looks comfy," said Mimi, and that made her feel a whole ton better.

WHAT HAPPENED AT DINNER

I was halfway finished with my supper when I remembered that Chip-Up was upstairs resting and I had forgotten to bring him down so he could eat too. It was really important to do the suppertime thing because that was one of the ways that Mom and Dad were going to see for themselves my responsibility.

"Oh, I see that Chip-Up is back," said Mom. Then Dad said, "A responsible dog owner wouldn't forget to feed her dog dinner." This was not something I wanted him to say, and I especially didn't want him to start using his favorite *irresponsible* word on me. So I said, "A real dog would be easier because he would follow me everywhere I went, and at suppertime he'd stand right next to me drooling, so I could never forget to feed him, even if I wanted to, which I wouldn't! Chip-Up is harder to take care of because I have to do all the owner stuff, plus then I have to remember to do all the dog parts too."

Mom was smiling and nodding her head up and down, which meant that she was thinking that I was 100 percent right. But then Dad said, "Well, that may be true, but you have to remember that there are many things that your Chip-Up doesn't do that a real dog would. Things like bark when you want him to be quiet, chew on things he shouldn't, demand to be taken out for walk . . . right?"

When a dad gives you a whole list of things you didn't think of before, it can be hard to think of the right thing to say back. Sometimes it can be so hard to think that your stomach, which was so very hungry before the list, now says, "No more food, please." This is what happened to me.

BACK TO MY JOURNAL, SORT OF

Dad has ruined all my filled-with-excitement feelings and good thoughts about the Chip-Up project. This is what I wanted to write in my journal, but then I remembered the part about Miss Lois reading it and I didn't want her to think Dad was mean and bad, even if I was thinking those things. I was feeling so yucky, I didn't even want to write about dogs at all, even though Emma was looking like one of the best dogs on the whole list and she was a small dog, so I should have been super happy. The other good dog was Mika, and of course that one was Mimi's favorite because she was big. It was hard to say anything bad about Mika because it wasn't her fault she had grown up to be big. If she were small I would have for sure loved her as much as I loved Emma. But I didn't feel like writing about any of this in my journal. Instead I wrote about the only thing that I didn't really have to think about, and it was for sure not going to be interesting when I was old and forgetting about my life now, but I didn't care.

Today I had toast with butter and jam for breakfast. I also had a half glass of orange juice, which is not my favorite, but Mom says I have to drink it because it is healthy. I just saw Mrs. Witkins climbing into her very own house through her basement window. This is weird because I can see her whole family watching something on TV upstairs, so it's not because she is locked out of her house.

MRS. WITKINS'S HOUSE

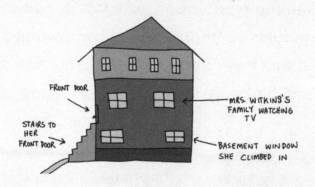

FRONT DOOR

STAIRS TO HER FRONT DOOR

MRS. WITKINS'S FAMILY WATCHING TV

BASEMENT WINDOW SHE CLIMBED IN

It was a good thing that I looked out my window when I heard Oliver bark, or I would have missed her. Mrs. Witkins lives next door to Mr. Hurley and Oliver across the street. Anytime someone steps even close to Mr. Hurley's house, Oliver starts barking. He is not very friendly, but he is a very good watchdog. Oliver must have heard Mrs. Witkins trying to climb in the window. Mrs. Witkins is a very nice lady, but she is not someone who you would think would be climbing through windows in the night. She is not very sporty. She is definitely not a rock-climbing-type mom or even a jumping-around-type mom. She is a sewing-and-cooking-type mom, so this was for sure something very strange that was going on.

OLIVER'S DREAM PRESENT

I watched for a long time, but nothing more happened except that Mr. Hurley took Oliver for a walk. Oliver loves to eat all kinds of garbage from the street, so Mr. Hurley is always trying to pull disgusting things out of Oliver's mouth before he can swallow them.

Mimi and I would have to be careful not to pick a dog like that. I watched for Mrs. Witkins some more, but I couldn't even see her in the basement, so it was kind of boring. Maybe she went out a different window that I couldn't see.

MR. HURLEY'S
HOUSE

MRS. WITKINS'S
HOUSE

Tomorrow I was definitely going to tell Mimi about Mrs. Witkins so we could both watch from our windows to see if she did it again. Then I drew a funny little comic for Mimi so we could remember about not picking a dog that eats garbage.

THE OTHER GRACE

Grace L. was looking at me again in class. I think either she really wants to be friends with us other Graces or she doesn't like me.

It's hard to tell, because she is not a very smiley-type person.

WHAT HAPPENED AT SCHOOL TODAY

Sammy Stringer said he is 100 percent going to bring his skateboard over after school today. That is good because then at least we can tape Chip-Up to it and take him for a walk. That'll be one of the new three things that Dad said a real dog would do. We'll have to make sure that Mom sees us so she can tell Dad all about it.

Mimi said that tonight we definitely have to watch and see if Mrs. Witkins climbs in

her basement window again. It happened around eight o'clock last night, so that is when we are going to do our spying.

Miss Lois reminded us that we must not give up on our journal writing. Then she told us about some famous people who kept journals and how those journals were important today because they told us things about history and life from a long time ago that we might not normally know about. Now we have cameras and video, so journal writing is probably not so needed anymore, but I didn't say that out loud because I could tell that Miss Lois would not be happy to hear it.

FAMOUS PEOPLE WHO HAVE DONE JOURNAL WRITING

Lewis and Clark were two really important explorers who traveled from Pittsburgh, Pennsylvania, by land all the way to the Pacific Ocean and back again. They were the first explorers to do this and it took them a really long time, almost three years. Back in 1803 when they did this there were no cars or railroads, and of course no planes, so they had to walk the whole way. They kept a journal of all the things they saw and all the adventures they had. This was important because when we read it today we can know what life was like way back then, since everybody from then is now dead and can't tell us about it.

Beatrix Potter, who was a famous writer and drawer of children's books, started a journal when she was fifteen years old and wrote in it every day until she was about thirty years old. The cool thing about her was that she wrote her whole journal in a secret code so that even if other people found it they would never be able to read it. I am sure she didn't use flashlight Morse code because that would have taken her forever and then she wouldn't have had time to write all her books. She wrote lots of stories with bunnies and little animals that had adventures and could talk, such as Peter Rabbit.

The last person that Miss Lois told us about was Samuel Pepys. She said he had one of the most famous journals ever. He lived in London, England, in the 1660s and kept a journal about everything that happened in his life. This was a big deal, because he wrote about the Great London Fire of 1666 and about the Great Plague of London in 1665.

Plague is a bad sickness that kills most people who get it. His journal must have been very sad because he was writing about a lot of dying. If I had to write about people dying I would for sure be crying. I wonder if his journal has tears on the pages. I was going to ask Miss Lois but was interrupted by Valerie Newcome, who started talking right away in front of me and didn't even put her hand up.

**ME GIVING VALERIE A MEAN LOOK BUT
I DON'T THINK SHE NOTICED**

Valerie Newcome said that journal writing was exciting to her because she was planning on being famous when she grew up, so her journals would probably be worth lots of money and be really interesting for everyone to read. Martin, the boy who sits behind her, said, "Famous for what?" But before Valerie could answer, Miss Lois said we all had to calm down, and she started talking about Samuel Pepys again, which was not as exciting as Miss Lois thought it was.

I stopped paying attention and started doodling, and I don't know why but it turned into a little cartoon about Valerie being famous. It wasn't a very nice comic, but I didn't really do it on purpose. It just came out that way.

Miss Lois saw that I wasn't paying attention, and before I could hide my paper she took it from me. The next words she said were the most horrible words you would never want to hear.

THE MOST HORRIBLE WORDS

Miss Lois said, "Just Grace, you will take this and report to the principal's office!" Mr. Harris is nice, but he's the principal so he is still scary, and it is especially no fun to sit on the black chair outside his office. Everyone who sees you there gives you the you-are-in-so-much-trouble look. Mrs. M. is extra good at the look, and this is especially bad because she is the office helper who sits right across from the black chair, so she can give you the look a lot!

WHAT MR. HARRIS SAID

Mr. Harris looked at my comic and said, "So, can you tell me about this?" I was glad to be able to do some explaining, because I wanted him to know that it was an accident and that I didn't really mean to be mean on purpose, and that maybe Valerie would be famous one day and then everyone would need to know that she used to make Barbie clothes out of see-through tape and somehow that would be important for history. I was happy when he said that he understood that part.

But then he said that the part he did not understand was why I was drawing a comic when I should have been paying attention in class. This was the part that I was not ready to do any explaining about, because you can't tell a principal that you think your teacher is boring.

So I said, "I'm sorry. I won't do it again." "Good, glad to hear it," said Mr. Harris. And then he said that he was going to throw away my comic so that no one else could see it, but that he wanted me to draw him a new one for the next day about something I had learned in class. Something about journals, and something that was not mean-spirited, which is a word that means making fun of people so they get their feelings hurt. Then he sent me back to Miss Lois.

SLOW, SAD WALK BACK TO MY CLASS

SOMETHING THAT IS HARD BUT NOT IMPOSSIBLE

It is hard to walk back into your classroom after you have gotten in trouble at the principal's office. It would be better if it was impossible—then you wouldn't have to do it—but it's not. Miss Lois said I could take my seat, and everyone stared at me as I did it! I kept my eyes looking at my desk for the whole rest of the time until lunch because I didn't want to see anyone looking at me.

As soon as the bell rang for lunch Mimi rushed over to my desk to ask about what had happened. I could have told her the whole long truth but I didn't. Instead I said, "I'm not allowed to doodle anymore while I'm in class." That way she didn't even ask about the comic, which I wished I had never drawn in the first place. Sometimes if you try

hard enough you can almost pretend something never happened, especially if there are
only three people in the whole world who
know about it.

ME

MISS LOIS

MR. HARRIS

CHIP-UP'S FIRST WALK

It was nice that everyone was so super excited about Chip-Up. It made it easier to forget
about my bad day. Max and Sammy watched
while Mimi and I did the taping of his legs to
the skateboard. And before we all left for the
park I made sure to yell to Mom that I was
taking Chip-Up for a walk. Chip-Up was easy
to pull because Sammy had a really nice
skateboard with good wheels. Sammy said

he wasn't sure if he was going to stay with us at the park, and I knew that was because he  was not happy about meeting any real dogs. I couldn't wait to introduce Chip-Up to Emma.

THE PARK

When we got to the park, none of the real dogs wanted to meet Chip-Up. They were all too busy chasing balls and playing with other real dogs. Emma wasn't there so I couldn't tell if she was going to be interested in Chip-Up or not. Sammy said he'd stay with Chip-Up if we wanted to go and visit with the real dogs, and I knew that was because he did not want to be near large furry animals. Mimi and I met three new dogs to add to our list but they were not as wonderful as Emma, or as smart as Mika, or as sweet as Winkie, though they were skinnier. The dog owners who we had met before were all happy to see us and were all talking together like they were the people part of the dog club. Two girls who were young like us were there too.

Their dog was just a puppy so they couldn't let him go off the leash because he wasn't trained yet and would probably run away. Dog people seem to be very friendly, maybe even friendlier than cat people, but that's kind of hard to tell for sure because cats don't really like to hang out with other cats, so their people can't hang out together either.

I DON'T THINK MY CAT LIKES OTHER CATS.

SO WE'LL JUST STAY HERE ALONE.

WHAT DAD ASKED FOR

On the way home I told Mimi, Max, and Sammy what Dad had said about Chip-Up not really being a very good example for taking care of a dog because he didn't do that many real dog things. "You need to make him more real," said Max. "Have him do more real dog stuff." "Maybe you should pretend harder," said Mimi. "You know, make it a bigger deal." Sammy didn't say anything, probably because he didn't want me to get a real dog anyway.

When we got to my house we took Chip-Up off the skateboard and I took him inside because it was suppertime, and supper-pretend-time with Chip-Up.

THE SHOW

All through dinner I did lots of talking to Chip-Up. I told him not to beg, I told him to sit (even though his legs didn't bend right so he couldn't do it anyway), and I told him to lie down and stop whining. I even made some whiny noises so it would sound more real. Mom was having a hard time not laughing, and that was okay because it was kind of funny, and all I wanted anyway was for Dad to be paying attention.

After dinner Chip-Up and I rolled around in the living room making lots of noise. Then Chip-Up jumped up on the couch and got in trouble and had to sit in the corner. This pretending was turning out to be a lot more fun than I thought it would be. I don't know why, but Chip-Up was in a very naughty mood.

When I wasn't looking—so
it really wasn't my fault
because I couldn't stop him—he went and
chewed up Dad's shoelaces.

He got sent to the backyard for that,
because as a good dog owner, which I am, I
know behavior like that is just not acceptable!

After a while I forgave him, and I'm pretty sure he knows never to do that kind of
thing again. I was having so much fun with
Chip-Up that I almost completely missed
looking out my window at eight o'clock. It
was good luck that I heard Oliver barking,
because that reminded me about it.

MRS. WITKINS

Mrs. Witkins was standing at the bottom of
her stairs, waving to her daughter Emily, who
is older than I am so we don't know each

other. After Emily closed the door, Mrs. Witkins started walking down the street, and I thought for sure she was not going to do the window-sneaking thing again. But as soon as she passed Mr. Hurley's house she turned back around and walked through his yard to get to her window. Of course Oliver was going crazy with barking. I was hoping that Mimi was looking because Mrs. Witkins is not a very good window climber and that made it 100 percent funnier to watch. Just like the time before, the last thing I saw was Mrs. Witkins's bottom disappearing through the window.

As soon as that happened I went to my side window to see if Mimi was there. Of course she was, and she was waving her flashlight around to try to get me to notice her. I turned my flashlight on and held Chip-Up next to me so she could see him.

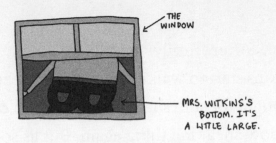

THE WINDOW

MRS. WITKINS'S
BOTTOM. IT'S
A LITTLE LARGE.

Right away Mimi started flashing her light to tell me she wanted to send me a message. I had to put Chip-Up down so I could write out the Morse code she was sending me.

It always takes me longer than it takes Mimi to figure out what a message says. I think my brain gets confused with all the dots and dashes. This time it took twenty-five minutes to figure out her message, but most of that time was taken up with looking for my Morse code chart, which probably got knocked off when Chip-Up fell off my window, because where I found it was under my bed.

WHAT MIMI'S MESSAGE SAID

Funny

Mostly I think flashlight Morse code might be just too hard to ever be fun.

WHY I CAN'T GO TO BED

Miss Lois was right: It's much easier to work on your journal if you do it the same time every night. I had a little thought that maybe I should write something nice about Valerie—that way when Miss Lois read it she would know that the comic I made was a mistake and that I wasn't trying on purpose to make fun of Valerie and that it was really just something that was unfortunate. But then that reminded me of the comic I still had to make for Mr. Harris. And since I couldn't think of anything special to say about Valerie that didn't sound dumb and not true anyway, I decided to write about Mrs. Witkins again instead. I was going to describe her house and where the basement window was, so I looked out and guess who I saw climbing back out of the very same basement window?

Mrs. Witkins is my across-the-street neighbor. Every night at around eight o'clock she leaves her house and pretends to walk down the street, and then she sneaks back and climbs into her very own basement window. At about 8:45 she climbs back out the window and goes up the stairs and into the house through her front door. She seems to be very sneaky!

I was hoping that Miss Lois was not going to think I was being mean by saying that Mrs. Witkins was sneaky. I on purpose left out the part about her being kind of tubby and having trouble fitting in the window, because it sounded like I was maybe making fun of her, and I for certain did not want to get in trouble again. Just thinking about being sent to Mr. Harris's office was making me all sad in my stomach again.

HOW TO USE A FLASHLIGHT AT NIGHT

Dad came into my room to say good night and said I had to go directly to bed because it was way past my bedtime and tomorrow was a school day. I couldn't tell him about Mr. Harris's comic because it is not a normal thing to have to draw a comic for the school's principal and he would have for sure been full of questions about wondering why.

If I did not have to, I was not going to tell him about getting into trouble at school. Girls who get in trouble at school do not get to have a present of a real dog in their life. I know that 100 percent.

After he left I put on my pajamas, made Chip-Up a bed on the floor, and said good night to Mom. I had to turn off my light because both Mom and Dad have light-bulb sensors in their brains. They would notice the light being on and catch me not sleeping in seconds. They are like superheroes about light.

MY JOURNAL COMIC

I made a tent with the covers over my head
and started to draw Mr. Harris's comic, using
my flashlight so I could see.

NOT A GOOD WAY TO WAKE UP

I got woken up this morning because I heard Dad yelling something about shoes. I was lying in bed thinking *shoes* sounds a lot like *snooze,* which was something I wanted to do more of because I was so tired from staying up forever drawing Mr. Harris's comic.

Then suddenly I remembered Chip-Up and his chewing. In half a second I was 100 percent totally awake. Now I could hear Dad really well. "Why are my shoelaces chewed up? Will you look at this? I can't tie anything with this half-chewed lace! Do we have squirrels in this house? What's going on? Now I'm going to miss my train!"

I could hear Mom too—she was trying to keep Dad calm. "I don't know, dear. Here are your loafers. Wear these. I'm sure we'll figure

it all out later. Have a good meeting, dear.
See you later." And then nothing.

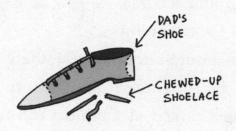

DAD'S SHOE

CHEWED-UP SHOELACE

THIS IS GOING TO BE A BAD DAY

Chip-Up and I went down the stairs really
super quietly. I had to carry him because he
makes a thump on each step if you pull him
with his leash, and you can't sneak around
with a thumping dog behind you. We went
outside and stood on the front lawn for a little while, and I sort of wished it could be forever because I did not want to go into the
kitchen and see Mom. Finally I had to be

brave and go back inside. Mom didn't say anything, and for half a second I was hoping  that she thought that maybe there was a squirrel in the house too. But that was before she looked at Chip-Up and me and shook her head in a way that said, *Boy, I feel sorry for you, because you are going to be in so much trouble!*

CAN I STAY AT SCHOOL FOREVER?

Mimi and I walked to school together. She didn't have any great ideas about how to save my life.

I gave my comic to Mrs. M. because Mr. Harris wasn't in his office. She gave me her you-are-in-trouble look. It was as if she could tell that all the unluckiness in my life was in no way nearly over.

It's really hard to concentrate when you are waiting for bad things that you know are for sure going to happen. Miss Lois could tell that I wasn't paying good attention because she kept saying, "Just Grace, are you with us?" I was trying to think of something super special and great to do so that Dad would have to 100 percent lose his angry feelings.

It's not easy to think of super amazing get-out-of-trouble ideas. I couldn't think of anything.

On my way out of the school I noticed that Mr. Harris had taped my comic on his door. This was a total surprise and it made me smile for half a second. It was one lucky thing in a very unlucky-looking day.

No Sadness For Me

All the way home Mimi and Max and Sammy wanted to talk about taking Chip-Up to the park. They were not filled with sadness like I was, and they did not have any sympathy for me. Sympathy is when you feel bad because someone else feels bad and you want to show you care about that. All they cared about were dogs.

I was surprised that Sammy even wanted to go back to the park. When we got to my house I tried to stay outside on the front lawn for as long as I could. Max finally said, "Come on! Go get Chip-Up so we can go." Mimi offered to go with me because it's a fact that a parent yells at you less if you have a friend standing right next to you. As soon as we walked into the kitchen, because Max and Sammy wanted us to bring a snack too, Mom said, "Your father is working late tonight." That was two lucky things. Now all I wanted was one more lucky thing, and that last lucky thing was a not-mad Dad.

THE WALK TO THE DOG PARK

We taped Chip-Up to the skateboard, gave out the crackers, and then finally we were walking to the park. When we walked past Mrs. Witkins's house, I totally remembered that I had forgotten to tell Mimi about Mrs. Witkins coming back out the window. So I told the whole story to Max and Sammy too so they would know what we were talking about. It's good manners to include everyone in a conversation if you can remember to do it.

Sammy said it would be cool if Mrs. Witkins was a spy. I said I didn't think she looked like she could do any cool spy stuff because even getting in the window seemed like it was hard for her to do. Plus, who would she be spying on, anyway? Her family? Sammy said, "Yeah, I guess you're right, but still, it would be cool if it was true."

He was right about that, but it was too hard to imagine that it could be true. Mrs. Witkins was definitely not like an M&M. She was not a superspy underneath and a regular mom on top. You could just tell about that.

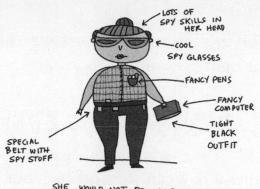

LOTS OF
SPY SKILLS IN
HER HEAD

COOL
SPY GLASSES

FANCY PENS

FANCY
COMPUTER

TIGHT
BLACK
OUTFIT

SPECIAL
BELT WITH
SPY STUFF

SHE WOULD NOT BE WEARING HER
FLOWER SWEATSHIRT, WHICH IS
HER FAVORITE BECAUSE SHE WEARS
IT A LOT.

IF MRS. WITKINS WAS A SPY

DOG THOUGHTS

"I hope Emma will be there!" I said. I wanted to talk about something that was 100 percent for sure good. "Me too," said Max. "Her owner said he's going to help me teach her how to do a flip." Mimi and Sammy didn't say anything, probably because Mimi was thinking big-dog thoughts, and Sammy was thinking no-dog thoughts, and both those thoughts were not really group thoughts right now at that moment.

THE WORST DOG EVER

Sometimes a day can start off bad, but then other things happen and you think that maybe in the end you will be lucky and it will not be so bad after all. This is the kind of day I was hoping I would get, but this was not what happened, because as soon as Emma saw Chip-Up rolling in the park, she attacked him!

First she tried to bite the skateboard wheels as I was trying to pull him away, and then she grabbed Chip-Up's leg. She had it in her teeth and she was shaking it so hard, she pulled him right off the skateboard. She would have run away with his whole entire body except that Sammy was brave and grabbed Chip-Up's middle. Emma was growling and we were all screaming—it was terrible! Emma had Chip-Up's leg in her mouth and no matter how hard Sammy pulled on Chip-Up she wouldn't let go. Finally she ripped his whole complete leg right off his body! Emma turned around and took off with it. Max tried to catch her, but she was too sneaky and speedy for him. She ran to the middle of the park and chewed it up until there was nothing left but little pieces of litter. I couldn't believe it! She was Horrible!

CHIP-UP'S LEG

WHO IS VERY SORRY NOW

Mr. Scott, who is the man that owns Emma, said he was sorry about a billion times and we could tell he felt really guilty that his dog had turned into a crazy, horrible creature. It took him forever to get Emma back on her leash. I guess her two favorite games are soccer and chase me. Max helped chase her down while Mimi and I inspected Chip-Up. We were too surprised about what had happened to even cry. Sammy went to pick up the little pieces of Chip-Up's leg because he is good about not littering, and all the dog park

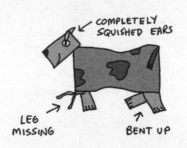

COMPLETELY
SQUISHED EARS

LEG
MISSING

BENT UP

people were coming over to us with their dogs and Sammy didn't want to be close to any dogs. Chip-Up looked terrible. His new name could be Rip-Up!

Mr. Scott offered to pay to get Chip-Up fixed, but since Mimi and I just made him out of cardboard we couldn't take any money. Everyone was super nice and trying to make us feel better with their words. Finally someone asked why we had made Chip-Up in the first place.

It was nice to talk about something different because all the sorry talking was starting to make me feel like I was going to cry. I told them about how Chip-Up was going to show my parents I was responsible and dependable, and once that had happened they were going to have to buy me a real dog.

I think this made Mr. Scott feel even

worse because he started saying "I'm so sorry" again. The man that owns Bernie said he had some ideas to help and that he wanted us to come back to the park tomorrow to talk about them. Mimi was holding Chip-Up and she was starting to cry, so we had to leave. It was a very sad walk home. By the time we got to my front door, I was crying too.

HOW CHIP-UP SAVED MY LIFE

Dad opened the door like he had maybe been waiting for me, and I guessed that he was, because he had his chewed-up shoelaces in his hand. What he saw was not at all what he had been expecting, because he dropped the shoelaces and said, "Grace, are you all right? Tell me what happened. What's wrong?"

And then I couldn't help it. I started crying so hard I couldn't even talk. Mom and Dad were really upset about Chip-Up. I was 100 percent surprised that they cared so much. They wanted to go back to the park and talk to Mr. Scott about Emma and her attacking ways. This was not something I wanted. Even though I was newly filled up with mean feelings about Emma, I didn't want her to get in trouble or have something bad happen to her.

It took a long time, but finally Mom and Dad said they would not complain to Mr. Scott. After supper Dad totally surprised me when he said he wanted to help me fix Chip-Up's leg. It was nice of him because he is much better at glueing and taping than I am. When Chip-Up had his parts all together again we put him on my bed. Then Dad said, "Now, Chip-Up, there will be no more shoelace chewing, or chewing of anything else in this house! Understood?" Of course Chip-Up couldn't say anything, so Dad looked at me. I was kind of too nervous to talk, so I just nodded my head up and down in the *yes* way. "Good," said Dad, and then he patted Chip-Up on the head, smiled at me, and left my room.

It is pretty hard for a dad to be mad at you when you are already crying really hard about another bad thing that has already happened, so I guess I was lucky about that.

MY CHIP-UP BAND-AID

He fixed everything for me.

EVERYTHING BACK TO NORMAL

At journal time I was looking out my window and watching Mrs. Witkins climb in her window again. Only this time it didn't seem so strange, because I was already kind of used to it and was expecting it. Right after Mrs. Witkins went in through the window, Mr. Hurley came out of his house with Oliver. I couldn't write about Mrs. Witkins again, so I decided to write about Oliver instead.

Oliver is a dog who lives right across the street from me. He lives with Mr. Hurley, who is his owner. Oliver does not like children, but Oliver does like to eat garbage he finds on the street. If Mr. Hurley let him, Oliver would probably eat all the garbage he found everywhere.

Mimi and I did not look at each other through our windows before bed. I was sort of glad about that because I was super tired and I just wanted to go to sleep. This is not something that happens very often. I even let Chip-Up sleep next to me, and this time he was hardly even pointy or in the way at all.

MY MORNING

At breakfast time Mom said she was happy to see that Chip-Up was back to normal. And even Dad said good morning to him. Somehow, it was weird to have Mom and Dad being so nice to Chip-Up. I couldn't tell if that meant I was closer to getting a dog or further away from getting a dog. Parents are hard to understand. Plus, the awful part was that if I was closer to getting a dog, now I

wouldn't even know what kind of dog to get.
Emma had ruined everything.

DOG PARK

Since today was not a school day, Mimi, Max,
Sammy, and I decided to go to the dog park
first thing in the morning. Of course we left
Chip-Up at home. We didn't want Emma to
stick her teeth into him again. Max said that
dog people like to walk their dogs first thing
in the morning, so he was pretty sure that
Bernie and his owner would be there. We

were curious with wanting to know how Bernie's owner was going to help us.

On the way we saw Mr. Hurley walking back with Oliver. We all crossed the street so we wouldn't have to walk by them because of Oliver not being friendly to kids.

When we got to the park the dog people were all talking together in a circle and they did not look happy and smiley like usual. Mimi said that it was probably going to be bad news for us, because Bernie's owner was doing some pointing, and his pointing was in our direction.

GOOD OR BAD?

WHAT WAS A SURPRISE

I was not wanting to have any more bad news in my life, so I said, "Let's just go home right now." I guess Mimi was thinking the same thing, because she said, "Okay." We were just starting to walk back when Max said, "Wait! They want us to come over. Look!"

We looked, and he was right: the dog people were moving their arms and hands in that come-over-here way. So we all had to walk over, even Sammy. "Sorry, kids," said Bernie's owner. "We've had some sad news. We were just talking about our friend August and his dog, Oliver."

I couldn't believe it. "Mr. Hurley's Oliver?" "That's right," said the man. "Well, I suppose you'd know him, what with you kids being so excited about dogs." "Well, we don't *know him* know him," said Sammy. "Oliver doesn't like kids." "Well, that may be true," said the man. "I don't know about that."

And then he told us the sad story of how Oliver was not eating his food anymore, and no matter what Mr. Hurley did, he could not get him to eat. And how Mr. Hurley was so worried that he was even making Oliver special meals of people food, but still that was not working either. Bernie's owner didn't say it, but I could tell that he was thinking that Oliver might even die!

Then he said, "Uh-oh, here comes trouble." And he was right. Trouble was running up to us at top speed. Emma jumped all over me like I was her fav-

orite person in the whole world and she had not only yesterday ripped the leg off of my special homemade pretend dog. It's surprisingly hard to be mad at a real dog when it is showing 100 percent love for you.

WHAT HAPPENED NEXT

Mr. Scott said that he was really sorry again, but this time it did not make me sad because Emma was licking my hand. Mr. Scott said that Emma was still young and she still had some things she needed to learn, and one of those things was to not chase skateboards. He said she loved to bite skateboard wheels and was probably so excited about the skateboard that she bit Chip-Up by accident and then unfortunately it just got worse from there.

I don't know why, but suddenly I was 100

percent forgiving her. Mimi did not feel the same, because when Emma came over to her, she just looked down at her and did not even give her a pat.

Mr. Scott didn't notice Mimi still being mad, because he said, "You kids are great. I want you to have these." Then he gave us each a free movie pass and some coupons for treats at the movie candy counter. Mimi couldn't be mad about that, and she wasn't, because now she was smiling too. I thought that was our big surprise, but then Bernie's owner said, "Do you kids want to hear my idea?" Of course you can't say no to something like that.

BERNIE'S OWNER'S IDEA

Bernie's owner's name was John. It was a lot easier to ask him questions about his idea once we knew what his name was. He told us what to call him after Max said, "Excuse me, Bernie's owner, do you mean you are going to pay us real money?" Max was asking that question because John wanted to know if we would walk his dog, Bernie, in the park on Mondays and Wednesdays after school. He said he had to work late those days for the next two weeks and would not be able to take Bernie out.

I couldn't believe that he was offering us a real job for money. And after he said he thought we were responsible and dependable, I totally knew we couldn't say no. John said that he lived across the street from the park so his house would not be hard for us to get to. Then the other dog people said that they would be there every day to help out if we had any problems. It was amazing. Suddenly we were in the dog club and we didn't even have to have our own dog.

PERFECT

On the way home I was so happy, I almost felt like if I tried it I would maybe even be able to fly. There was no way that Mom and Dad could say that I was not 100 percent responsible and dependable if I had a real job. Plus, the job was going to be amazing practice for when I got my own dog. It was so, so, so perfect! Mimi was happy too. She said she was going to save up all her money and buy something really great. She didn't know what it was going to be yet, but it was going to be fantastic. Max said that he was going to try to teach Bernie a new trick as a surprise for John when he got back. The only person who was not excited and not saying anything was Sammy.

MOM AND DAD HAVE IDEAS TOO

Mom and Dad were even more surprised about the idea than we were, and they were full of questions, because it is not every day that you get to have the most perfect job in the whole world given to you as a surprise. It was lucky that John gave us a note to give to them, because after a while I got tired of answering all their questions about it.

Dad called John on the phone and made a plan for us all to meet the next day to go over what we would have to do on Monday. Mom let me break the rule about no phone calls after 8:00 p.m. so I could call Mimi, Max, and Sammy to tell them about it. Sammy was the only one who didn't sound excited. I told him he had to come but that he did not have to touch Bernie if he didn't want to. Even then he did not sound very happy or filled with joy.

WHAT I FORGOT ABOUT

I could hardly wait to work on my journal and write down all the things that had happened, because these were not things I wanted to forget about when I was old and couldn't remember anything. It was going to be fun to read all about my first job, that part I was sure of.

Today the most amazing thing ever happened and it was right when I wasn't expecting anything. John, who is one of the dog people, offered Mimi, Max, and Sammy and me a job to do dog walking. The two great things about this job are that we get paid and that it proves that I am responsible and dependable at 100 percent. Mom and Dad will get me a dog for sure!

I was just finished writing my journal when I heard Oliver barking. I couldn't see Mrs. Witkins anywhere, but then I saw Mr. Hurley walking down the steps with Oliver. The next thing I thought in my head was the perfect idea to help Mr. Hurley, and that is because my empathy power was just suddenly working.

My thought was "Poor Oliver, if only Mr. Hurley let him eat garbage. Then he wouldn't die from not eating." This may not sound like an amazing idea, but it really was, and it was an idea that could save Oliver's life.

I ran downstairs and made Dad come across the street with me so I could talk to Mr. Hurley. I was a little bit scared because I knew that Oliver didn't like me, and Mr. Hurley does not seem super friendly either. But when you are using your superpower,

you really can't worry too much about stuff
like that.

**MY EMPATHY SYMBOL IF I HAD A
SYMBOL LIKE SUPERMAN'S**

AN IDEA THAT COULD SAVE A LIFE

I decided to say the idea really fast—that way
Dad and I wouldn't have to stand there, with
Oliver not liking me, for very long. So I said,
"Mr. Hurley, I think you should try hiding

Oliver's food outside on the street. That way when you take Oliver for a walk he will think it's garbage and eat it." Mr. Hurley was totally surprised! He asked me what my name was and then he said, "Grace, I don't know how you thought of it, but I think I'm going to have to try your idea right now. If you'll excuse me, I have some food to hide. Thank you so much for thinking of Oliver."

Dad and I walked back to the house and Dad was looking at me like he was surprised too and he said, "You know, when I was a kid I really liked dogs too." This was a great moment, because Dad's non–animal person outside shell was suddenly peeling off, and he didn't even notice it yet.

I DO LIKE DOGS.

WHAT MR. HURLEY DID

I went upstairs and spied on Mr. Hurley from my window. I wanted to see if he was really going to do my idea. If I didn't know what he was doing, I would have said that Mr. Hurley looked like a big litterbug! He was walking around outside dropping food in little piles on the sidewalk and by the curb. After he was finished, he brought Oliver out. At first I couldn't tell what was happening or if it was working, but then when Mr. Hurley walked under one of the streetlights, I could see that he was smiling. Oliver was truly a garbage-loving dog. He even loved pretend garbage.

For the second night in a row I was super tired. Maybe all this thinking about real dogs was more work than just thinking about

Chip-Up. Poor Chip-Up—he didn't even get to go outside today. I was hoping Dad wouldn't notice that part.

JOHN'S HOUSE

John's house was right across the street from the park just like he said it was. Before we got there Dad told us that we had to be serious about our new job and that meant no fooling around. We all said yes, we knew that already, but I was still thinking that Bernie would probably like it better if there was at least a little bit of fooling around.

When we got there Dad and John did a lot of talking. At first it was sort of interesting stuff, but then it got really boring once Dad found out that John was a guy who knows a lot about trees and plants. Dad had all sorts of questions about how to fix up our yard, which I think looks perfectly fine just the way it is.

I was happy when John had the suggestion of us taking Bernie for a practice walk in the park while he and Dad watched from his front porch. Bernie is a good dog to practice on because he doesn't pull on his leash or want to chase squirrels or skateboard wheels. I was surprised, but I was liking Bernie a lot more than I thought I would.

Before I knew him, I would never have put his kind of dog, with little stubby legs, on my list of dogs I liked. But after spending time with him I could tell that if I had a dog like Bernie, I would love him very much. The most fun part was holding the leash, but I was good about it and let Max and Mimi have turns too. Sammy didn't want a turn at all.

WHO IS GOING TO DO IT

Everything was going perfectly, and then all of a sudden Bernie pooped. Mimi said there were poopy bags on the leash holder, so that was lucky, but someone still had to pick it up. I didn't want to do it because I didn't have my rubber gloves with me. Mimi was holding the leash so she said she couldn't do it. Max said it was too stinky and he might throw up if he got too close, so he couldn't do it. None of us wanted to do it, and the worst thing was that Dad and John were watching us. If we didn't pick it up they would for sure take our dog walking job instantly and completely away from us.

Then Sammy said, "Boy, you are such a bunch of babies. I'll do it." And he pulled out the poopy bag and walked over and picked it up. It was like he was our surprise hero. Mimi even said a little "Yeah!"

WE DID IT

When we got back from the walk, Dad and John were still forever talking about trees. They said that we had done a great job, and this meant that we could keep our dog walking job, which was really good news. I couldn't tell if they knew that none of us wanted to pick up the poop. Hopefully they were too busy talking about trees to notice. Sammy had turned out to be a super-big helper on the dog team, even when he didn't like dogs!

John showed us where he hid his front door key so we could get into the house on Monday to pick up Bernie. And Dad made us all promise that we would not go poking through John's things, which we wouldn't have done anyway because we know it's not nice to be nosy like that. I almost couldn't wait for Monday to come.

On the way home Dad told us that John was a landscape architect. A regular architect is a person who draws designs so that people can make houses. A landscape architect draws where the grass and trees and rocks and bushes go. Dad said it was a very interesting job to have, but it didn't seem very exciting to me.

When we got back to my house we all sat together on the front lawn. Dad went inside but then he came back with a box of cookies. Max said, "Your dad is the greatest," which is mostly true, but he was not the greatest because of the cookies, because the cookies were not even from him.

There was a note on top of the box that said, "For Grace. Thank you, A. Hurley." Nobody saw the note but me, which was good because I didn't want to do a bunch of explaining about why Mr. Hurley was giving

me a box of very delicious cookies to eat.
Sometimes a person just gets tired of explaining stuff.

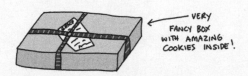

VERY
FANCY BOX
WITH AMAZING
COOKIES INSIDE!

WE ARE TRULY HAPPY

Max was super excited about our new job.
He said when we had finished working for
John we could make posters, and then we
could do the dog walking job for other people too. It was so amazing to think that we
were doing this great new thing. Even
Sammy was excited.

I looked across the street to see if I could
see Mr. Hurley. I kind of wanted him to see

how much we were all liking his extra-delicious cookies. He wasn't there, but someone else was watching us, and I was 100 percent completely surprised that it was Grace L. She was sitting on the front steps of Mrs. Witkins's house, which is not a place I would ever think I would see her. Mimi saw me looking across the street, so she did too. Pretty soon we were all staring at Grace L., who was staring right back at us. I started to feel my guilty feeling again. It was the same guilty feeling that I had pretended to ignore when I was sitting with the other Graces and Grace L. was watching us. It was the kind of feeling that could make my tummy say it did not want anymore supertasty cookies.

"I wonder why Grace L. is sitting on Mrs. Witkins's steps," said Max. Then without thinking I said, "Let's find out," and I moved my arm and hand in that come-over-here way.

ONE LAST MYSTERY

Grace seemed a little shy at first but that was not for long. We had so many questions and such delicious cookies that she forgot about the being-shy part pretty fast. The reason we had so many questions is that she knew exactly why Mrs. Witkins had been sneaking into her basement window at night.

Grace L.'s mom is friends with Mrs. Witkins, which is why Grace L. was sitting on the outside steps. Mrs. Witkins was inside, showing Grace's mom a quilt she was making for her daughter Emily's birthday, which was in a couple of weeks. She wanted the quilt to be a surprise, so every night she left the house, saying she had to go to a meeting or shopping, but instead of going anywhere she snuck back inside through the window and worked on the quilt in the basement.

Grace said Mrs. Witkins had a huge bruise on her leg from falling through the window. She told us Mrs. Witkins had said, "It's not so easy to climb in and out of windows when you are old."

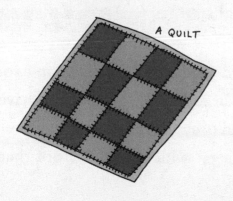

A QUILT

Sammy said he was a little disappointed that Mrs. Witkins was not a spy but just a sewing-loving person instead. Still, it was pretty cool that she was working so hard to make a nice surprise for Emily. Grace L. made us promise not to tell anyone about the quilt, because if Emily found out about it before her birthday, Mrs. Witkins would be 100 percent heartbroken. We all promised not to say anything, and I was pretty sure Sammy would keep the secret, because after Grace L. left he asked me what a quilt was.

MY LAST JOURNAL WRITING

I passed Dad on the way to my room and, feeling brave, I said, "Dad, can I have a dog?" He didn't say yes. He didn't say no. He said, "We'll see," which is total proof that his outside shell is breaking. If I weren't so tired I would flashlight Morse code Mimi all about it. Now all we have to do is pick out the kind of dog we want. This is not so easy, and it will probably take a long time, because dogs are a lot like people. There are a lot of M&M's out there. At first their outside seems like one thing, but then when you get to know them, you find out that underneath they are something else.

Mrs. Witkins was like a professional spy tonight. She disappeared into her basement window as quick as a flash, and that was because she had a new mysterious stool under the window to help her. Mr. Hurley dropped more litter around the neighborhood, and Oliver was happy about that. Chip-Up is sleeping on my bed again, and he looks just perfectly happy with his head on my pillow. Even though I have a job with a real dog, I'm going to keep him for a while, at least until I get my real dog, and I can just tell that's going to be happening pretty soon.

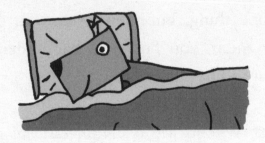

I had to write five sentences in the end because sometimes you can't say everything you need to say in just four sentences. I was sure that Miss Lois was not going to mind. She was a teacher and teachers all liked stuff like extra writing. Plus, it was nice to tell her how everything worked out—that way she wouldn't be wondering about it, because everyone likes to know how a story finishes at the end.

DOGS I WOULD NOT WANT AND WHY

Dear Miss Lois,

If you want to give me some extra marks for doing this extra part for my project then I will not be unhappy about that kind of thing happening.

SPANIEL (CLUMBER)

This kind of dog comes from England, which is a place I would like to visit, mostly because they speak English there and that would be helpful when you are on vacation. I read that these types of dogs drool and snore. This is not something I want to be happening at night when I am sleeping, especially if I let the dog sleep on my bed with me.

DOG HAS REALLY SAD EYES. ALWAYS LOOKS UNHAPPY

BEAGLE

This is another dog from England. It is a very cute dog, but it has a very power-ful nose. Once it smells something it likes, it takes off and chases that smell, and even if you call it and call it, your dog will not come back. I do not want a running-away dog!

EXTRA-GOOD NOSE

PLOTT

This dog comes from the United States so you might think that it would be perfect for me, but that would not be true. It is the kind of dog that loves to hunt and chase bears. I hope to never have

TRAINED
BEAR HUNTER

bears near me, so this is not the kind of dog I am needing.

CHINESE CRESTED DOG

If there was an award for strangest-looking dog, this is totally the dog that would win. It's mostly funny-looking because it doesn't have hair on the main part of its body. It's the kind of dog that you have to dress in clothes or else it will get cold when you go outside. It

would probably be a good dog for
Valerie because she likes to make outfits.

KOMONDOR

This is a dog that looks like a giant
mop. You can't even see its face.

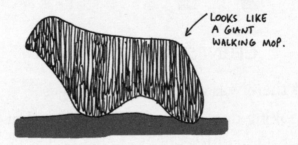

LOOKS LIKE
A GIANT
WALKING MOP.

This is the end of my report and most
of what I know about dogs that would
not be right for me.

Charise Mericle Harper is the author and illustrator of many books for children, including the Just Grace series. In a starred review, *Booklist* called Just Grace "hilarious," and said, "The kids come alive in the story, and Harper enhances the comical goings-on with sparkling cartoon sketches. Give this to . . . anyone looking for a funny book." Charise lives in Westchester County, New York. Visit her website at **www.chariseharper.com** and visit the Just Grace website at **www.justgracebooks.com**, where you'll find all sorts of fun things, including videos, quizzes, and information about all the Just Grace books.

Ready for More?

Check out these other series from

HOUGHTON MIFFLIN HARCOURT!

Meet Gooney Bird Greene!

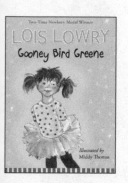

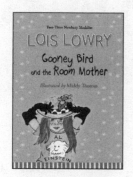

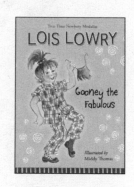

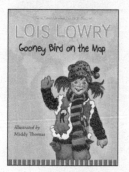

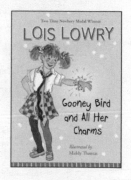

When life gives you lemons, make Lemonade!

The Anna Wang Series

Anna and her friends show how friendship can cross cultures!